Of Saints and Miracles

a novel by **Manuel Astur**

Translated from the Spanish
by Claire Wadie

NEW VESSEL PRESS
NEW YORK

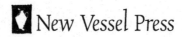
New Vessel Press

www.newvesselpress.com
First published in Spanish as *San, el libro de los milagros*

Copyright © 2020 by Manuel Astur
The English edition is published by arrangement with
Manuel Astur c/o MB Agencia Literaria S.L.
Translation copyright © 2022 Claire Wadie

The translation of this work was supported by the Peirene Stevns Translation Prize
which was established with the generous support of Martha Stevns in 2018.

Library of Congress Cataloging-in-Publication Data
Astur, Manuel
[San, el libro de los milagros, English]
Of Saints and Miracles/Manuel Astur; translation by Claire Wadie.
p. cm.
ISBN 978-1-954404-06-9

Library of Congress Control Number 2022931702
1. Spain—Fiction

CONTENTS

"It is out of love for the source that the stream flows away to become a river, estuary, ocean, salt, blue, song."
— CHRISTIAN BOBIN

"Animals do not gaze at the stars; animals know nothing of stars. We have all the stars."
— ELIAS CANETTI

For Sara, my mother, and Raquel, my fellow traveler:
my xanas, *with you I can unravel*
any golden thread without breaking it.

First Song

THE KILLING

We are the first words. We've been here before yet we've only just arrived. We are fiesta days and working days and dog days. We are the one who sets you alight and the one who puts out the flame. We are the one who wakes you in the morning, and the one who leaves you shattered in your bed at night. Naturally, we are the one who then steals your sleep. We are the enemy and the only solace. A whisper. A fistful of words, the last words.

We nearly kept quiet. First, we played for time. When the time came, we hesitated. It was never the right moment. In the end, we said to ourselves: no, this is the right moment, because it is all moments. We have the voice and we have the time.

We have all time.

* * *

Just as a sun-soaked stone radiates heat for a while after nightfall, there is a point on still summer evenings when objects appear to shine, as if to give back part of the generous daylight they've received. In such moments, Marcelino would stop what he was doing—clod of earth on the hoe, spade sunk deep in the hay, scythe dripping with fresh green blood—to stand up straight, wipe his brow with the back of his hand, and contemplate the valley below. Everything would be gleaming, chiming like a bell of golden light. He would let his eyes fill with sky.

And so, as the sun set on that July evening, Marcelino stopped and contemplated. The house, the stilt granary, the cart with its shaft reaching skyward, the dry straw, the ears of corn, the cows in a single spine coming home along the track, the dog's bowl, the rusty drum among the nettles, the axe in the tree stump, the woodchips and the logs, the sawdust on the ground, even the moss that hugged the stones in the walls of the small vegetable plot, even the trees in the nearby woods and the mountain peaks: everything shimmered, silhouetted against the deep blue sky, in which a single bright star heralded the coming of a new age. Everything, that is, except the large bloodstain in the sawdust, and his brother's body, both so dark they seemed to trap the light, as if the black ink that was slowly flooding the valley was seeping directly from them, saturating the sky and sketching the shapes of bats, which began to dance around the yellowish light of Cobre's lone streetlamp.

The truth is, he'd never meant to hurt him.

It had happened once before, when he was a boy at the school in Villar where everyone used to call him stupid and a cowshagger. They would screw up their faces and open their mouths wide in strange expressions that reminded him of horses and that look they have. At the same time, they would point at him and make grunting noises. Until one day he grabbed hold of one of them to make him stop, and it turned out that the boy's bones were as fragile as a sparrow's. Even though he'd never meant to hurt—afterward, his father hurt him a lot more—on that occasion it worked out for the best, because he got expelled and never had to go there again.

This time, however, it would turn out for the worse. For sure.

He'd spent several days chopping up a plum tree that had fallen in the last storm. His brother arrived, red-faced and sweating from his climb up the path that led from the road to the house, and sat down on a tree stump. He was wearing a hideous polyester suit and carrying a battered briefcase. The wax in his hair had melted, he was sweating so much, and the long strands he had as usual combed over his bald patch had flopped sideways, forming a strange tonsure and making him look like some kind of medieval monk who got off on holding a burning candle to his balls. Without bothering to say hello, and still breathing heavily from the massive effort of dragging all that weight up the hill, he opened the briefcase, took out several papers with wineglass stains on them, and handed them to Marcelino, who looked at them like a little child staring blankly at a dictionary.

"Yes, yes, you're an animal, you can't read, I know. It doesn't matter," his brother said, getting to his feet. He looked in the briefcase again and took out a pen, which he also passed to him. "Just sign here and here and I'll leave you in peace."

Marcelino stood there, papers in one hand, pen in the other, utterly bewildered.

"All right, you fucking retard, just scribble down four of your shitty letters and job done. Or put a cross. Do whatever the fuck you want. But do it now, because I haven't got all day," he said, sitting back down on the stump.

Marcelino drew some shaky forms more akin to prehistoric hand paintings on a cave wall than writing.

"There you go, good boy, that's the spirit." He put the documents in the briefcase, got up, swept his hair across the bald patch and turned to leave. But then he stopped abruptly, as if something had occurred to him.

"How can I put it, Lino . . . These papers, the ones you've just signed, they state that you agree to settle the mortgage." He hesitated. "No, hold on. It's more like these papers state that everything you own, everything that used to be ours, inherited from Mother and Father—the house, the meadows, the granary, the vegetable plot, the cows, the lot—no longer belongs to either of us, but to some nice gentlemen who will come to claim it in the next few days. Do you understand what I'm saying?"

But Marcelino didn't understand. His brother took a hip flask out of his inside pocket and took a swig, as if feeling a slight pang of shame or guilt. The stench of alcohol on his breath smothered the scent of earth and fresh grass. He seemed to battle with himself, before making up his mind:

"Listen, shit for brains. You've got no house, no meadows, no cows, no vegetable plot, nothing. It's all gone. So start packing up your crap, and when they come, get the hell out, because they won't tell you twice and I don't want any trouble. Do you understand?" He took another swig.

And that's when Marcelino punches him.

His brother lets go of the hip flask, puts his hands to his head and pats it gently, as if someone's messed up his hair. When the realization hits, he looks at Marcelino as if seeing him for the first time, frowns, more puzzled than angry, and rolls his eyes inward to look at himself for the last time. He collapses.

A great red river runs down his forehead, bends at the bridge of his nose and then forms a lake in the corner of his eye, flows across his cheek, and seeps into the white linen of his shirt. A sound escapes his half-open mouth: not a moan but a gurgle, like a drainpipe. Marcelino's dog, a red-coated mongrel, barks.

* * *

"Ino, Ino!" his brother called out.

His brother must have been six years old at the time. He was a sweet child. Marcelino loved giving him piggyback rides and would do so whenever he was asked, even if it made his back ache. It was before he started hitting Marcelino, back when he still admired him and wanted to spend all his time with Lino, as he used to call him. His brother had a vivid imagination and was very smart. Lino could spend hours listening to the fantastical stories he invented.

Lino was taking a moment to sit and rest in front of the house; his father had just left for the bar. It was getting dark, and the clouds were so red that it looked as though the fields behind the mountains were ablaze. A chorus of little frogs was celebrating the return of the cool evening air.

"Ino!" his brother shouted, rushing up and jumping on him. Lino laughed.

Taking him by the hand, his brother pulled Lino toward the grain store; beneath it was a wooden cart. He pointed to one of its wheels, crouching down to look at something.

"*Mine*, Ino."

It was big and hairy. Gigantic, evil. The creature was as ugly as its web was beautiful, swaying gently in a breeze so slight only the spider could feel it. It ignored them, counting microscopic coins with its tiny feet. Lino's brother spun around to face him, his eyes shining with excitement, as if he'd found a diamond.

"Pretty!" he cried joyfully.

"No, it's ugly."

"*Noooo*, pretty!" he insisted.

Lino gave in. "Yes, it's pretty."

He named it Lina, in Lino's honor; he said it reminded him of his brother. Lino wasn't going to argue. He loved that little boy more than anything in the whole world. Lina only survived a few days. One morning the web was gone and she was nowhere to be seen, and his brother cried.

A few years after that, the little boy disappeared too, and Marcelino was left all alone. He didn't cry then either.

* * *

There once lived an old woman and an old man who had nothing to eat but a piece of cheese.

Along came a mouse and ate the cheese that was all the old woman and the old man had to eat.

* * *

And on those summer evenings you could almost see the shadows growing longer. It was as if the day were stepping back, quietly heading home after a good day's work. And even once the valleys were sated with darkness, the mountaintops would still catch the last of the golden light, like islands in the middle of immense black lakes. And then came that time of evening when the first streetlamps in the village—points of yellowish light dotted here and there—flickered before finally coming on while the sky was still blue, and you felt more keenly than ever the brush of the earth against the heavens.

From Marcelino's house, the lights in the village resembled a serene and wistful little cluster of stars. As you looked up from the valley, the lamp outside the house that was still Marcelino's, almost at the top of the mountain, was the last to light up, at the same time as Venus.

* * *

San Antolín is the capital of the municipality of San Antolín, which covers an area as large as London or Madrid but has only six hundred and twenty-four inhabitants, according to the census. According to the census because half of them, the half under sixty, have moved away and only come back for holidays.

You might have heard of the place because of the Neva nature reserve, named after the river that carved out most of the valleys. Or else for its well-preserved little villages, or, more recently, the sanatorium and spa where it is rumored that the late Prince of Asturias, Alfonso de Borbón y Battenberg, a known hemophiliac, spent long periods of time before giving it all up to become the prince of partying and madness. It is also known for its eternal silence and eternal bad weather, although this particular aspect isn't exclusive to the area.

The large number of fortified settlements unearthed by amateur archaeologists shows that the area has been inhabited since pre-Roman times, and yet in all its history it hasn't produced one single figure of note. Determined not to be outdone by their neighbors, the locals erected a bust of their own in front of the town hall, an early-twentieth-century schoolmaster whose only claim to fame was that he managed to teach a few kids to read and write without ever beating them.

Despite the fact that San Antolín was a fifth-century French martyr and is a well-known patron saint of hunters, the parish church is dedicated to San Antonio, the patron saint of animals. No one ever appeared to see the irony.

You can reach San Antolín from the south, from the Leonese mountain pass at La Grada, by negotiating your way along twenty-five miles of bends and steep drops. Or from the north, where at Villar you can come off the fast and convenient motorway which runs the length of Asturias, offering glimpses of the Cantabrian Sea, and drive along a regional road for about seven miles, following the river Neva. This is the preferred route for both the young locals making their escape and the tourists flocking in. These visitors usually turn up in full mountaineering gear, as if they're about to scale the Himalayas rather than simply eat a *Flecha de San Antonio*—a sweet, arrow-shaped treat, a specialty in the area—down a few ciders, and buy some local handicrafts.

Admittedly, the impression that you're leaving the real world behind can be uplifting. You might almost imagine these tiny villages with their limestone houses and slate roofs as a stage set placed there purely for your entertainment. Especially when, having passed through miles of forest and valleys so steep that the sun's rays don't reach the ground, the road opens out into the vast light-filled valley that San Antolín shares with two hamlets: Carriles and Cobre. The second of these, perched almost at the mountain's summit, like a kite surveying its territory, consists of just three houses, two of which are abandoned, their roofs sunken like saggy old cushions.

In San Antolín there is an ironmonger's that sells farm equipment, a supermarket, three cider bars, a cake shop, six souvenir shops, and two hotels. It boasts a town hall and a police station; a community center with several tables, some packs of cards, and a few books; and a doctor's office that opens for appointments on Thursday mornings. Parked at the taxi stand are two vehicles which, along with a rickety old bus that comes in from Villar on market days, service the whole municipality. There used to be a primary school, but it's been decades since there were enough children, and the few there are usually board in Villar, otherwise they wouldn't be able to attend school in winter because of the snow.

Broadband arrived eight years ago and there's been cellphone coverage for ten, although there's only one network. Privately owned television companies didn't move in until 2002.

* * *

When Marcelino was a boy, all the fields were kept neat and tidy. He remembers the families hard at work on the land at this time of year, reaping and harvesting the fruits of the earth. The men cutting the tall grass in neat semicircles with their scythes. The women and children behind them arranging it in rows so that, days later, it could be piled up around wooden posts driven into the ground. The seeds floating in the golden air. That was the Old World, which had disappeared, along with most of the villagers. There was no laughter to be heard now, and almost all the neighboring fields had been abandoned to the forest. The only noise you heard these days was the occasional distant hum of an engine, one of the villagers cutting his fields with a mower, as if there were any reason to rush. Given the chance, Marcelino would have single-handedly looked after all the pasture as far as the eye could see. He would have cut the grass with a scythe, repaired the fences, and filled the meadows with gentle cows so that the twilight hours could once again echo with the deep and calming chime of their bells—an age-old sound that had all but disappeared, leaving the hills orphaned, overrun with ferns and vermin.

Marcelino was slowly moving through the meadow, opening a path with his scythe: it was entirely up to him now to keep the chaos at bay.

He caught the sound of a cow bellowing in pain somewhere in the distance and straightened up.

* * *

He stroked her head to calm her. The other cows carried on eating, oblivious to their companion's condition. Marcelino inserted his hand into the large vulva and pushed until his whole arm was inside the cow. He felt for the calf, which was wriggling deep inside, and made sure it was the right way up. Luckily everything seemed to be in order, so he withdrew his arm to let nature take its course while he reassured the mother, a large mottled cow, Marcelino's favorite, for which he felt more affection than he ever had for any woman who was not his mother. As night began to fall, the tiny trembling calf tried to pull itself upright.

Marcelino could have gone home and come back in the morning, but some time ago the wolf, who used to exist only in legends and ghost stories, had returned to reclaim his kingdom. It was not unusual to hear howling at night, especially in winter, when the wolf strayed into the villages in search of food—a chicken, a calf, a sheep, even a dog. And so, even though it was a still, warm evening, he lit a fire. He ate a few blackberries he'd picked from the hedgerows. He drank milk straight from the cow, his head beside the calf's, and then smoked a cigarette. He slept soundly, and woke only twice to check that everything was as it should be.

* * *

Sofía doesn't know how old she is. She can hazard a rough

guess, because she does know that she was born during the last war, but she's not quite sure when that was.

Her birth certificate was destroyed in a fire or misplaced. Either that or her father never even registered her arrival—because he had better things to do than waste two days trekking over the mountain to Rodiles and two days coming back just to record that he'd had another child, when this one might not live more than a few months either. In any case, her ID card has a random date on it. The true mark of her birth is a small scar, a patch of stretched, hairless skin on her right temple, which she'll happily show anyone who's interested.

As she tells it, when "the Galicians and the Moors" arrived, her entire family fled to the forest. She was a baby, and her sister, Remedios, who would've been no more than five, carried her in her arms. The Moors were shooting and the Reds were firing back. Nobody cared that it was the middle of the night and that the village, with most of its inhabitants sound asleep, was in the direct line of fire. Outside, in the forest, bullets were whizzing all around her, tearing branches off the trees. When they eventually reached La Cuevona, her mother got a fright because Sofía was covered in blood. But she calmed down when she realized the bullet had only grazed the baby's temple. Any further in and she'd have been dead. An inch or so the other way and it would have killed her sister.

"It was a miracle," she says, rearranging her hair and gently smoothing it down. "So you see, that's when I was born, and my sister too. We were born at the same time."

What she does know is that she wasn't born here. Sofía was born in San Andrés del Monte, about seven hours east on foot. Beyond the four houses that make up the hamlet of La Condesa. Even beyond the Guanga sierra. In a sun-drenched village on the slopes of Bueymuerto. A proper little village, complete with an *indiano*-style mansion—built at the turn of the twentieth century with a fortune acquired in the Americas—a church, and, of course, a bar, all three of which have fallen into ruin and been swallowed up by the undergrowth, the one remaining inhabitant having died thirty years ago. Now it is a ghost town because, with no residents and no votes to be won, no politician has ever bothered to convert the dirt track into a road or have electricity brought in. And so the village has been condemned to fade away along with the Old World, caught between two front lines for the second time. Sofía is the sole survivor.

* * *

Every summer, Sofía sets off and keeps on walking until she reaches the village where she was born. It sounds incredible, because her back is so crooked that when she walks it looks as though she's ploughing the earth. But it's true, as any of the rare hikers who make it as far as San Andrés del Monte will tell you. The cemetery is in ruins. A wall of burial niches collapsed some time ago, laying bare the cells inside, like a giant abandoned honeycomb. First moss, and then grass, have blurred the outlines of the graves. The tombstones are pages written in ink long since faded; stories that cannot be read. Two stone angels, swords in hand, stand guard over a preposterous mausoleum, final resting place of the owner of the grand *indiano* house. Their noses have crumbled away and their eyes, blackened by the passage of time, are dead, empty sockets. From a distance you can barely make out the cemetery at all; it's drowning in nature, foaming bubbles in every shade of green. But you can see three headstones, weathered yet gleaming white: two belonging to her parents and a smaller one, a mound of earth marked with a stone and a white wooden cross. This is the grave of her firstborn, a baby for whom she still weeps sixty years on, whenever a fever or too much alcohol brings her down. Her old house looks well-kept too. Small, humble, freezing, but with the windows intact, the roof still in one piece, the weeds kept at bay and the little doormat, like a faithful old dog, waiting by the door.

How must she feel when, all alone, she enters the ruined landscape of her memories? Which ghosts might she greet as she walks into the village? Who waits with open arms to welcome her? What goes through her mind as darkness falls, as she sits in her little chair in front of the house, a candle beside her and countless shadows lengthening all around? Perhaps she can see it all as it once was. Where you might see a tiny village square overrun with brambles, shells of houses on three of its four sides and a stone drinking fountain used only by the occasional wild horse, perhaps she sees the young men sitting on a bench outside the bar after work, having a glass of wine, cracking jokes and flirting with the girls.

"You're looking gorgeous, Sofía!"

Maybe there are children playing, shrieking with excitement. Cowbells chiming as the cattle come home, in glorious harmony with the bells of the little church ringing out across the valley. The crickets and the frogs in the river, the cuckoo, and the dogs barking because they're afraid the disappearing day will never return. The men's shouts and the thud of dominoes on the tables in the bar behind the yellow windowpanes—a puppet theater. The oil lamp casting the shadows of the men's heads onto the wall, prisoners trying to break free. The women on the doorsteps, catching up on all the gossip. Perhaps all of them, and all these things, are still here today; perhaps they linger on because she is here, remembering them.

Just picture her, sitting in her little wicker chair, in front of her old house. She says that when she dies she'd like to be buried here, with her family; her children are at their wits' end. One of the grandsons has come up with a plan to have her cremated and take her ashes to the cemetery. They might even scatter some in the village square. They haven't told her yet, but they're all agreed.

* * *

Marcelino ventured down the hill from Cobre only now and again when he needed something. But he didn't go to the market; he preferred to avoid people. He didn't like to go into San Antolín either, choosing instead the bar in the neighboring hamlet of Carriles that sold a few essentials for the old folk who didn't have anyone to look after them.

When he came back to the house that morning, he milked the cows and went down to leave his churn by the roadside, to be collected by the truck that came once a day. The few euros he got for the milk were his sole income. He was surprised to find that his brother's car was no longer parked at the junction. Retracing his steps, he discovered that neither his brother nor the axe remained on the ground by the woodpile. He guessed he must have gone into the house, furious, looking for him to get his revenge. There were finger marks in the thick dust on the furniture, like the footprints of tiny animals chasing each other. The wardrobes were open, revealing yellowed decaying rags that had once been clothes. His brother hadn't bothered to shut the drawers, and their contents—lifeless objects like screws, nails, pieces of wire, knife and fork handles, corks, and light fittings—resembled the rusty entrails of a bad memory. Panic-stricken, he lifted a floorboard and took out the metal box where he kept his most treasured possessions: an Astra pistol from the war; a silver-plated knife in the shape of a fish; a photo of his mother holding his brother, standing next to his father, whose face had been scratched away with a key; and a thousand euros in small notes, which he'd been saving these past years to buy a mule, partly because he needed one and partly just because he liked them. Everything was as he had left it; his brother hadn't found what he was looking for.

This time, Marcelino couldn't go to the bar in Carriles, because he was almost certain that his brother would be there, drowning his rage with alcohol. There was nothing for it but to go down to the bottom of the valley, to San Antolín, where, as usual on a Sunday, it was market day.

* * *

The way into San Antolín was across a stone bridge over the Neva that was only wide enough for one car, which meant that there was always a small traffic jam. But aside from the occasional toot, which if anything sounded jolly, as if a child on its father's lap were playing with the horn, no one complained. No one was in a rush. Why would they be?

A tiny cloud floating in the blue sky seemed to magnify its vastness. The light was so sharp and clear that even the short-sighted could see without glasses. In the distance, the rocky white mountain ridge towered, majestic and indifferent. At its feet, all the little valleys lay curled up together like puppies. A few old women were standing chatting next to a large wicker basket containing their wares: a handful of surplus vegetables from their own modest crops. There were two or three gypsies selling underpants, and plastic shoes that would fall apart as soon as you started wearing them. Several black men cheerfully displayed supposedly handcrafted leather belts and bags, which smelled as though they had come straight off the poor cow's back. We swear there was even a stall selling cassette tapes, and people were buying them. The bars were full to bursting; the terraces were packed, and some customers had taken bar stools out onto the pavement, which was littered with a snowfall of crumpled napkins and toothpicks. They were all talking loudly and gesticulating. Even the most wretched of souls seemed happy, and they all carried on as if they were immortal, which in that precise instant they probably were.

All except Marcelino, who hugged the walls, trying to pass by unnoticed, scared they might try to speak to him, say something that he of course wouldn't understand. It was always the same. They would open their mouths wide as if to bite him, wave their arms around, and screw up their faces. It seemed to him as if their eyeballs might fall from their sockets at any moment and roll around on the floor, and then what would he do, what could he do, someone as stupid as him, who didn't understand anything?

So Marcelino went to the ironmonger's, *La Llave*. He liked it in there because Artemio was a man of few words. Also, he liked all the tools and other objects that were crammed onto the shelves, floor to ceiling. Tools, unlike humans, don't lie. They are honest and their purpose is clear. What's more, they're not bothered who uses them, provided they are used for the job for which they were made. He bought an axe, a few nails, and some boxes of matches.

Then came the hard part. As fast as he could, he raced up and down the supermarket aisles, searching for the same items he always bought (for some reason, they were always moving things around and putting up huge posters as if it were fiesta season): four boxes of María Fontaneda cookies, the only treat in an otherwise bland diet ever since Olvido had introduced him to them when he was a child; five nine-hundred-gram cans of tuna in sunflower oil, the only fish he ate (plus, the empty cans had lots of uses); a few bars of Lagarto soap for washing both himself and his clothes; five kilos of pasta; ten cans of tomatoes; a five-liter can of olive oil; three kilos of flour; a few packets of medium roast ground coffee; fifteen loaves of bread; and three kilos of chorizo. María, the cashier, tried to make small talk, like she did with all the customers, which was why everyone liked her; but Marcelino looked down at the floor and didn't respond.

He took a taxi for only the third time in his life: the first was when he had to take his mother to the emergency room in Villar because his father had completely lost it; the second was when they buried her.

* * *

There were multiple tire tracks in the mud in front of his house, convincing him that his brother had returned, most likely with some friends, the ones with whom he'd just as readily drink himself into a stupor as go out hunting. They had rifles and were more vicious than the wild boars they left with their tongues lolling, bloody fist-sized holes in their flanks, tied to the trailers containing their frenzied dogs.

His brother must be furious. This time, simply looking down at the floor and waiting for the dark clouds to open wouldn't save him.

* * *

At the bar in Carriles, Marcelino didn't need to say a word for Pando Chico, the landlord, to pour him a glass of DYC whisky. It was what he ordered every fortnight when he dropped by, but he never drank it. It was a ritual, almost like lighting a candle when you enter a church. He sat on a stool listening to the ice cubes in his glass cracking like gnashing teeth before melting away. Four men were playing cards at a table. Pando stood leaning against the counter, reading the paper.

The stuffed boar's head above the fireplace surveyed the scene, its glass eyes yellowed by time and smoke. Not from the hearth, which was never lit, but from the millions of cigarettes and cigars consumed by successive generations of villagers. And that was fine. Nothing ever changed. Any changes would've put off the regulars, as well as the ghosts who were still there, chatting about the same old things.

He pictured his father sitting on a stool near him. He was smiling. He was nursing a glass of whisky too. His mood hadn't yet turned sour. He hadn't drunk too much yet and his soul hadn't blackened yet either. The flushed cheeks above his thick beard were a sign that he was content. He went to take out his cigarettes and Marcelino leaned over to offer him one of his. His father took one and smiled. Then he raised his glass in a toast. Marcelino did the same. No one paid any attention.

* * *

"They're looking for you, Lino," said Pando, when Marcelino went to pay for his drink.

The card players glanced at him.

Pando hesitated. Eventually he added: "Your brother."

It was enough to confirm his fears.

And that was the last we saw of Marcelino the Nobody.

* * *

Early the next morning, when the day was no more than a haze of light silhouetting the mountains, José Luis, already at work at the Mayjeco bar, brought in the empty bins, turned on the lights, unloaded the cups he'd put in the dishwasher the night before, wiped down the bar and tables with a cloth soaked in cheap gin, switched on the coffee machine, and, while he waited for the first customer—most likely Chitina, who went to work each day in Oviedo and got up as early as a nun—smoked a quick cigarette and read *La Voz de Villar*. There was only one news story: Manuel González Álvarez, of San Antolín, had been found dead outside his family home by his girlfriend. She had gone out looking for him when it got late and he hadn't come home. Now the police were looking for the victim's brother, who they feared might be injured. José Luis looked around for someone to tell. When he realized he was the only one there, he shook his head and tutted. He thought it was too bad, but something like this was bound to happen sooner or later. Then he thought how strange it was that in a place where nothing ever happened, two people should have died in the same week: barely four days ago the old spinster Benjamina's gas oven had exploded, taking Benjamina with it. When it rains it pours, he said to himself absentmindedly, using one of those clichés we tend to fall back on. He went outside and arranged the two tables and five plastic chairs on the terrace. The click-clack of Chitina's high heels echoed through the silent streets, waking up the entire village.

* * *

But if there was one thing Benjamina wasn't, it was an old spinster. She was old, certainly. And a spinster. But not the two together. Nothing about her suggested a woman who always wore black, or who whiled away the hours staring out from her little shack, pining for the life she could have had if only a man had loved her or she had let herself be loved. And there was no reason to imagine her grieving for her barren womb, which had never been blessed by the saints despite the countless hours spent kneeling, most of them praying at San Antonio's feet or scrubbing the church floor, eyes shining with devotion, her shriveled fingers counting rosary beads as if they were coins to pay Charon with, so that he would carry her from this valley of tears to a heaven conjured up from a whole host of paradises, fear, and ignorance.

Not a bit of it! That old spinster was not Benjamina. The real one wore clothes as flowery and vibrant as the blooms that trailed over almost the entire front wall of her house. And they used to say that as many men had passed through her bed as had visited the brothel in Villar, and that there wasn't a single man born between the 1920s and the 1950s within a twenty-mile radius who hadn't had filthy dreams about her.

* * *

"Let a man inside you a second time and you'll never get him out," she used to say.

* * *

You see, she'd had to turn down so many marriage proposals that the pumpkins she'd given, as custom dictated, to her disappointed suitors would have made a ton of "angel hair" jam—incidentally, the only part of the angels she was interested in. And to top it off, she had even seduced two or three grateful generations of one family, all of whom turned up at her funeral, barely able to conceal their smiles.

* * *

It is absurd to think yourself superior simply because you are alive. The arrogance of the present makes no sense whatsoever.

You already existed thirty thousand years ago. Those cave men and cave women dressed in animal hides, huddled around the fire, caked in mud and lice-ridden, were physically and mentally the same as you. The Mesopotamian farmer who at forty was the oldest in the settlement, and the priest who tended the eternal flame in the temple—neither was any different from your friends. The Egyptian pharaoh who had a colossal pyramid built, his very own space shuttle, which on his death would launch him into the stars to be united with his fellow gods—he could be your brother-in-law. The thousands of Romans, cheering excitedly as lions tore apart Christian virgins in the arena—they were all of us. And that torn-apart Christian virgin was our sister, and we the ones who later made a saint of her. Nothing, absolutely nothing, differentiates us from the millions of Germans who worshipped Hitler, or from the Russians who let communism get out of hand. Nothing distinguishes you from your grandparents, who believed themselves superior too. You are your forebears in the Plaza de Oriente, mourning the death of Franco, and you are the liberals shouting "Down with NATO." You are, and you will be, the same: all convinced that you are unique and superior for the simple fact of being alive. You will be your children believing their own technological lies, and we will be our grandchildren frying our brains with drugs yet to be invented.

* * *

But let us continue. We have the voice and we have the time. We have all time. This is the moment.

* * *

Along came a cat and ate the mouse that ate the cheese that was all the old woman and the old man had to eat.

* * *

We were just saying that Benjamina would always say, before hawking up a big gob of saliva and spitting it out between her teeth, "Let a man inside you a second time and you'll never get him out."

Like a climber who freezes to death in a cave on K2, doing what they love and the only thing they know, that is how Benjamina died: having almost reached the summit of her insignificant life, free and beautiful like the porcelain thimbles she collected.

She liked to drink La Asturiana anis; classic or cherry. She loved big hearty meals and sleeping in till lunchtime. At the age of eighty she would get dolled up as if she were a twenty-year-old going to the *romería* festival. She hardly ever travelled and never left Spain. She didn't like the city and she refused to fly. She didn't like foreigners either, although she was prepared to make an exception for the black men who called at her door now and then selling trinkets.

Once a month her only nephew, a dull forty-something who lived in Oviedo, would come for a visit. She would sometimes joke, when she was trying to endear herself to him, that she was so alone she could drop dead and the neighbors wouldn't even notice until she began to smell. But in truth she was only alone when she wanted to be, and she wasn't alone at the end. The kitchen exploded, the roof blew off, a huge blast shattered the glass in the neighbors' windows, a shower of tiles rained down on the village, and the column of smoke could be seen from Villar. Even El Sordo, deaf as he was, got to hear about it. It was a gas leak, at dinner time.

The fiestas that are held in villages and hamlets throughout Spain, generally in honor of the local saint, usually culminate in a spectacular display of rockets and fireworks. And it was the same for Benja. The explosion that echoed across the whole valley was the firework display that brought her magnificent fiesta to a fitting close.

After the fireworks, the decorations are gathered up, the stage is dismantled, and all the families, and all the youngsters who have drunk too much, go home.

"God must be a man," Benjamina once said, drunk on anis.

* * *

Early one morning Lino heard his father calling for him.

He found him by the creek. He had pruned the hazel tree, almost to the ground. Its supple, slender branches, lush as a peacock's tail feathers, lay in an enormous pile.

His father told him to pick off the hazelnuts, put them

in a basket, which was almost as big as he was, and peel the stems. And to not so much as think about eating any nuts.

He set to work. Happily, at first. The soft white down from the undersides of the healthy green leaves drifted in the clear sky, landed in his hair, covered his clothes like light filtering into newly opened, still sleepy eyes. The bark of the straight stems peeled off to reveal their fresh, shiny, smooth insides, like a tooth peeping out from a child's gums.

As time went on the feeling of happiness wore off. His hands hurt from tugging at this hard, flexible wood, which he just couldn't pull apart. The down formed a sticky film with his sweat, and his face itched no matter how much he scratched it.

Midday came and he was hungry and he was only a child and he couldn't eat the hazelnuts because Father had forbidden it and the beatings hurt even more than the hazel stems.

And midday went, the afternoon was ebbing away, and still he kept going, almost buried in leaves, there beside the creek. The sun began to sink between the mountains and puffed itself up like hens do when they're about to go to sleep.

At the sound of footsteps he looked up to see his mother coming toward him. She handed him a piece of bread and butter; the rye bread looked like caked mud. Lino sat down among the leaves and ate. His mother watched him and then her gaze shifted to the mountain of hazel stems beside him, and the basket filled almost to the brim with nuts.

She praised him, and he promised her that he would be finished by the time Father came back.

After he had eaten he let out a great belch, which made his mother smile. She took a handful of nuts from the basket and gave them to her son.

Lino ate them, and his mother collected the shells. As she left, she kissed him on the forehead.

* * *

His father returned when the full moon was high in the sky. Lino was asleep on top of the mound of leaves. After checking that the task had been completed to his satisfaction, his father lurched drunkenly, picked up one of the stems, and whipped him awake.

Lino sat up. His father loomed over him, a gigantic dark shadow stinking of alcohol. A swarm of flies was buzzing around him. Lino picked up the basket and put it on his shoulders. It was bigger than he was, and he felt his bones bend under the massive load. His father watched him for a few seconds and laughed. As they walked he carried on beating Lino with the stick, as if he were a mule, but when they reached the house he didn't hit him with his fists, and let him sleep in peace.

* * *

But that was the Old World. In the New World it was getting dark when Marcelino arrived home. He fed the cows and gazed at the newborn calf, which was sleeping beside its mother. Outside, frogs were croaking, crickets were chirping in the warm night air, and some dogs were barking farther down the valley. A cool breeze rustled through the branches of the hazel trees and swept into the cowshed, causing the little bulb, which shone with a faint yellow light, to swing gently. He felt very sleepy. A mix of emotions had tired him out and left him almost unable to sleep the previous night. He settled down on a pile of straw and simply dropped off, like a child.

* * *

He was woken by the nervous clucking of the chickens in the coop. Stepping outside, he inhaled the sharp breath of dawn. Night's black tapestry was unravelling, retreating to the top of the mountains, which were silhouetted by a blaze of pale light. He scratched the back of his neck. Then he brought the cows out and set them free.

All seemed to be fine in the henhouse. He opened the door so that the birds would escape once they realized that they could, which might take a while and would probably happen by accident, given that they are fantastically stupid.

He emptied a potato sack and packed it with food. As soon as there was enough light in the sky, he set off for the Old World.

At the top of El Barco meadow he turned to look at his house for the last time. A wash of gray watercolor was swirling out of the chimney. His mother was at the front door, his brother in her arms. He pointed toward Lino and they both looked at him. They were smiling and waving goodbye. He kept walking.

* * *

He remembered the oldest old man in the world, back in the Old World. He was sharpening his scythe, sitting beside a stilt granary, its old frame as tired and crooked as the old man's. His beret was so dirty that it looked gray. He had greeted Lino and his mother fondly. Lino must have been five years old. If he'd been a little older he might have walked the whole way, his mother wouldn't have been so tired, and perhaps it wouldn't have taken them three days to get there.

They had stepped into a whitewashed cottage with tiny windows, as dark and melancholy as the old man's eyes. He remembered too the small kitchen with its enormous hearth, individual outlines blurred by a blanket of soot covering absolutely everything. Over by the fire, the oldest old woman in the Old World. She was dozing in a little wicker chair; there was barely anything of her and she had such trouble breathing she'd probably have been better off dead. His mother gave her a kiss on the cheek and she opened her eyes, which were blue, almost white, veiled by thick cataracts. His mother stroked the old lady's cheek, and she caught hold of her hand, clinging on tightly, as if it would save her from drowning.

Lino's mother told him to give the little old lady a kiss. She smelled of cookies, earth, and bleach. Then she gave a toothless smile like a baby magpie and made a gurgling sound as if she had sand in her throat. She gurgled some more and his mother understood, even if he didn't. That was about all he could remember of the Old World. The yellow smell of human piss and past lives filled with misery. A white washbowl with a tear-shaped chip in its enamel, glowing in the darkness like an apparition. A one-eyed ginger cat asleep at the old woman's feet. A tatty old oilcloth on a rickety table. A few empty hooks, blackened by grease over the years. A handful of dried ears of corn tied up in a piece of cloth. Shadows dancing on the filthy wall. That's about it. Except that for once his father was far away. That's about it. Except that, that night, he slept beside his mother and felt no fear. Except that he was happy in the Old World, and that he now meant to go back. This time to escape from his brother. He kept walking.

* * *

Four hours later, at the Castañedo de Judas, he stopped. These four giant hundred-year-old chestnut trees—burned-out and hollow after countless lightning strikes and just as many fires built by shepherds who'd sheltered there—marked the farthest from home he had ever ventured on his own. They were so named not only because of the profusion of wizened branches, which were like brittle arms, but for the dark holes in the bark that resembled furious faces or witches' toothless mouths, or black satanic eyes, or the gates of hell where Judas was still burning along with all those who had committed suicide, and all the other wicked people, like José el de Cachulo, the priest, and Marcelino's father. But Marcelino of course didn't see any such faces or symbols of damnation. These were four fine chestnut trees. They would yield good chestnuts to be roasted on the fire for the whole family, and people would tell amusing stories, tinged with regret because the days would be getting shorter and colder, and the pregnant bears would be settling down to sleep in their caves and the wolves and the wild boar and all the other animals would be searching for somewhere to hide in the piles of dry black sticks the forest would soon become. The chestnut was a fine tree, full of warmth, closeness, and family. And someday these trees would be firewood, a yellowish wood not as hard as oak but tough, rich, and dense—the kind that makes the best furniture. Someday they would be charcoal, ashes. He kept walking.

* * *

What we grow upward, we must also grow deep down. A tree without strong roots is destined to fall at the first gust of wind.

While it may be true that all those who have had a miracle befall them prayed for it, it doesn't follow that praying is enough on its own. And while it may be true that all those who have achieved something wished to achieve it, it doesn't follow that simply wishing is all it takes. The past is village folklore, a fairy tale rewritten every day to get us through the winter, and to help us imagine a vast world beyond the valley. And the future is a promise in whose name we deny ourselves the one true paradise: this very moment we are navigating, as if on a floating island; this time in which we are living. Here, hovering a few inches above the ground—this is our kingdom. We are safe here. You see, it doesn't take more than that. This is the moment. It is all moments. We have the voice and we have the time.

* * *

And it didn't take much more than those languorous dog days of August. Some of the fields neatly cut for the last time that year, great bales of hay piled into stacks; others abandoned, their grass grown tall and yellow; treetops beginning to fade, earth loose and dry, waiting for a shower or a storm; the sparrows plump; the fireflies brimming with light. The days are long and full, like a siesta after a hearty meal, like a pre-Romanesque church dedicated to a god who is relatable, rural, benevolent, and not to be feared. And it seems as if everything will stay like this forever, even though the sunsets, turned golden by the caramel days, are becoming tinged, almost imperceptibly, drop by drop, with the silvery gray of the trout's back that is winter, and the swallows are disappearing unnoticed, until one day we'll realize they're gone, like a pleasant dream we forget on waking. And the god Pan, satiated with lovemaking, plays a melancholy tune on his pipes, and it sweeps through the forests and villages in the form of a breeze, trailing a handful of dry leaves behind it. And we wear a rueful smile, like a teenager who has lost his virginity to a girl he doesn't much care for, but hey, it is what it is. And we laugh as darkness falls and our laughter drifts up to the sky, transformed into bats and swirling plumes of cigarette smoke.

It didn't take much more than those dog days—drifting, directionless—for a story that should have died a death in the crime section of the local paper to be given a new and remarkable lease of life.

Not one, not two, but three of the papers stacked up in piles outside Ana la Colorines's newsstand were sporting front-page headlines declaring that Marcelino had killed his brother and then gone shopping.

This was the seed that began to grow over those lazy, humdrum August days; the tiny spring that was joined by so many other waterways that, together, they burst through the serene dams of summer.

* * *

The patches of sky he could see above his head between the chestnut and hazel branches were the color of dying embers, and the night shadows were already lying in wait along the wayside. For twelve hours he had been following the course of a tiny stream as small, insignificant, and pig-headed as he was and whose name, if it ever had one, had never been written down and had been lost when the last man to care a jot about it died. Marcelino had listened to it murmuring by his side all day, asking to be noticed, and so he decided that he would pay it some attention and moved closer. He drank from the stream's cool black ink. Afterward he leaned against the grassy slope of the riverbank to rest. He could smell darkness, stone, toad, placenta, life. He fell asleep at once, so he didn't see them approach.

* * *

"Isn't that him, only in disguise?" asked the younger of the two. "Look at his hair, his eyebrows, it looks like him."

The other one moved closer to Marcelino and peered at his face. She admired his eyebrows, like prickly chestnut husks, his hair, black, dirty and thick like a wolf's, and his thin lips and gentle expression.

"No, it's not him. Feel his warm breath. This man is mortal and he's sleeping because he's tired," she said, returning to the water. She was holding a baby barely a couple of months old at her breast.

"How long is it since we saw one?"

"I don't know. Ages."

"I'd begun to worry there were none left."

They were naked and standing up to their ankles in the water. Their skin was white with glints of green. The older one had hair the color of the earth; the younger one's was green. The baby bit his mother's nipple, causing her to cry out in pain. She took him off her breast and the baby began to cry, revealing shiny white teeth. A few drops of blood fell from the mother's nipple and transformed into tadpoles as they broke the surface of the water. The younger one looked at her pityingly.

"Perhaps his family is nearby. You might be able to exchange your child for one of theirs."

The older one said nothing for a moment and then shook her head.

"No, I don't think so. He's not wearing a wedding ring and he's as filthy as a dog. This man always sleeps alone. He's afraid and he's running from something. He could be a vagrant, a madman, a werewolf," she explained to her sister.

But her sister wasn't ready to give up hope yet.

"And do you think he could—" she started to ask, opening her hands to reveal a large skein of the finest gold thread.

"Don't be a fool," her sister interrupted sharply. Then she said, "Forgive me, I shouldn't have insulted you, I know you're only thinking of me." She took her sister's hands and closed her fingers around the skein like a flower. Then she pulled her out of the water.

They moved closer to Marcelino.

"Look at his hands, look at his fingers, they're thick and hard like the tree roots in the riverbank. Fingers like those could never unravel it. They'd break it as soon as they touched it. And we'd be responsible for the death of a man who's never hurt anyone. His heart would stop beating, the world would be a little colder, and we'd be to blame."

"But maybe—"

"Hush now, let it go," the older sister interrupted for the second time. "This child will die, like the others. This child will return to the earth, like the rest, whether we like it or not. And then the he-goat will find us, make us love him once again, with his laugh, his breeze, his sun, and his music, and everything will begin again," she said as they stepped away and their voices became once again the trickle of water across the stones.

* * *

Marcelino woke with a start and grabbed the pistol. As he surveyed his surroundings, he and the intruder spotted each other at the same time. A little fox with a bushy golden tail was holding his ground on the bank, barely two yards away. Marcelino smiled and put the pistol away. The fox carried on drinking. A patch of milky moonlit sky was just visible between the trees, above the stream. An owl hooted. His father had hated owls, because people said that when someone was about to die an owl would hoot outside their house at night. But his mother had explained to him that the bird was playing a flute to guide the spirits in the dark, and Marcelino liked that.

* * *

Pan, he of the goat's hooves and horns, fell madly in love with a nymph called Syrinx. She didn't share his feelings, so she fled to prevent him from possessing her. But he, in his desperation, pursued her across mountain slopes, lakes, forests, summits, oceans, rivers, into caves, he pursued her over land, water, and rock, through pollen, soil, and leaves, through blood and sap; he chased her through fog, through drought, through blackened forests, over the entrails of half-eaten animals, over semen, stripped-clean bones, and burned-out woodland, over snake holes, dried leaves, and rotten trunks, over the bellow of the rutting stag, over sharp fangs; no matter where she hid, he always found her and she was forced to escape all over again.

And so Syrinx, driven to despair by this relentless pursuit, begged the gods to help her hide from Pan. They took pity on her and transformed her into a reed growing beside the river. Along came Pan, having followed her tracks. But, for the first time, he could not find her.

Sadly, he cut a reed growing on the riverbank to make himself a pipe, and began to play a tune. The instrument he invented is known as the panpipes and is also sometimes referred to as a syrinx. Syrinx is also the name given to the vocal organ birds use to produce their beautiful song.

* * *

Some of the old folk in San Antolín still remember the story of that sleepyhead Pachín el Dormilón.

One day Pachín was cutting the grass in a meadow near the forest, not far from El Portón field, when he heard some sweet, beautiful music that sounded like many flutes accompanied by a thousand singing birds. Then a group of dancing young women appeared. They were so lovely he tried to get closer to speak to them, but suddenly all the strength in his body vanished and he slumped against a tree trunk, falling fast asleep. When he awoke, night was beginning to fall and his skin felt cool, like his newborn son's. Back at home, he called to his wife to tell her about what he thought had been a dream, but he couldn't find her. Worried that something had happened to her or to his son, he went to ask his neighbors; but on his way out of his house he noticed an elderly man whom he had never seen before sitting by the front door. He asked after his wife and son, and the elderly man looked astonished. Pachín told him about the dream he'd had a few hours before and the old man's face went white, as if he'd seen the Devil himself. Eventually the old man explained in a trembling voice that he was Pachín's grandson, and that it wasn't a few hours that had passed but a hundred and fifty years.

* * *

"The dead live in the clouds, Lino," the Reverend Father used to say. "Up there is Paradise, where the poor in spirit, the wretched, and the pious go." He would add, "You'll go there too if you're a good, obedient boy," pointing to the gray sky.

And Lino would gaze upward and nod.

* * *

But the clouds lie low in the North. The mountain peaks often sink their fingers into them; even so the clouds just as often drag themselves along the ground, drenching everything they touch, like a tongue, like incense in a frozen temple. Like a fog so thick it's no longer even a fog; so thick that the dogs cannot hear themselves bark. When this happens, time vanishes, and the old folk say that on those muddy paths you're likely to run into a neighbor who died centuries ago but doesn't know it. Which is why, whenever they cross paths, especially on days when the clouds bear down on the earth, countryfolk greet each other with their heads lowered and their eyes fixed firmly on the ground. Any little stream can flow into this riverbed, carved out by millions of feet, by thousands of insignificant lives that have come to an end or perhaps exist all at the same time. The boundaries are blurred, and for this reason the people from the North are not very religious. They live inside religion itself. And their religion is familiar, whimsical, small and practical like a stilt granary. Its legends and its saints fit neatly into a cart, into a basket woven from hazel stems.

But you hardly ever see those far-off clouds that you get farther south in the Meseta, sailing like ships in the blue sky. Those immense horizons, which make you feel small and want to seek refuge in a solidly built Romanesque church, don't exist here. Around here, if someone tells you the dead live above the clouds, you go and take a look. If some halfwit priest tells Lino that Paradise is in the clouds, he will go up to check. All he had to do was climb to the summit. He saw the washed-out blue sky, and beneath him a gray desert, with not a living soul there. And the cracked dry earth, the ferns, the brambles, and the scraggy dry grass bore no resemblance to the Paradise he'd heard about.

* * *

No, the dead are much farther away; or they remain among us; or they are us.

* * *

A few long-haired brown cattle were grazing freely on wild pasture with no fences or pens. There were a few semi-wild horses too; small, strong, and short-legged. At last, Marcelino had reached the summit. This time there were no clouds, and beneath him countless valleys unfolded, each split into large swathes of forest and thousands of squares of meadow, a patchwork quilt fashioned from scraps of green. And on the horizon a thin hazy line, the Sea. Marcelino was seeing it for the first time in his life.

* * *

"Lick, Ino," said his brother, holding out his forearm. He had been to the beach on a school trip and had just gotten home, ecstatic.

Lino stuck out his tongue and licked. He pulled a face, which made his brother laugh. He said it tasted salty.

"Yes, the sea is salty, very salty. You can't drink the water."

Lino nodded.

"And also there are really big waves that knock you over when you go in and it's so much fun and they make a noise like this . . ." and he roared. "And there are really high walls too, made of rock, and the sea crashes on them."

Lino nodded.

* * *

The earth was constantly flowing and changing, and the sea, he imagined, was unchanging, solid, immense, permanent: so he waited with bated breath to hear the sound of the earth breaking against the sea, of large pieces of rock falling from the walls, the rumble of huge chunks sliding down slowly, inexorably. But all he could hear was the wind, and the chime of cowbells from the hillside.

Though he didn't know it, the spring he paused to drink from was the source of the little stream on whose banks he'd slept the previous night. The little stream that flowed on, joined by other little streams on the way, until it reached the Neva, which in turn spilled out through a great estuary into the sea. He couldn't have imagined how something so small, by teaming up with all those channels and bodies of water, could become so immense. But he was even less likely to understand how such a ridiculous little thing had managed to bore through the rocks and the earth, wearing them down over hundreds of thousands of years to form the valley in which he lived. Although if he had grasped it, if someone had explained it all and helped him to understand, he would have appreciated the pigheadedness that allowed something so insignificant to change the world.

He kept walking until he reached the far side of the mountain, from where he could see the rocky mass of the Cantabrian Mountains. They shone serene and magnanimous under the sky, whose blueness verged on white. Behind him lay the infinite sea, the water you couldn't drink. Ahead, rock and ice. In between, life. The only one possible. The world no more than a whisper.

* * *

The Reverend Father became one of the dead himself, years ago. But if Heaven did exist, in the clouds or on earth, he wouldn't have found eternal rest there.

* * *

According to some scholarly types—seen as lunatics or sages, depending on the times—the spirits, be they fairies, gods, demigods, or rock stars, are possessed of neither flesh nor bone, neither hair nor cells. They are, in fact, immaterial. It seems they are composed of an energy that adopts whatever form humans believe them to have. This would explain why their appearance evolves over centuries and across cultures, and why there are regional and national differences. They are made up of a cognizant matter that responds to the collective subconscious. Just as clay takes on the shape of the hand that molds it, they reflect who we are at any given moment.

We ourselves are the apparitions.

* * *

And to top it all off, the word is that after he went shopping

Manuel Astur

he didn't hide back up in the mountains, as you might expect, but spent the night in his house, as if nothing had happened!

Jofer, the mayor, tried to hush it up, but it's all around the village already, and poor Matute, the local police officer, has to deal with not only those few villagers who are up in arms, but all the rest of them making fun of him.

Juan el del Rusco thinks Lino didn't do it, and if he did, it was in self-defense, because his brother was a nasty piece of work. Gerardito says what's unbelievable is how the village idiot is making idiots of the police. The other regulars, who are enjoying it all so much they haven't even taken the dominoes or cards out of the box, are divided into two camps: those who think Marcelino hasn't got a clue what he's doing, and those who say he's as wily as a fox when he wants to be, and that no one'll catch up with him in the wilds.

By afternoon, the mayor is left with no choice but to give his first press conference.

* * *

Marcelino could just make out the rooftops between the trees. The village looked as if it were stretching out a hand, like a body buried by a green avalanche. The path was hidden by undergrowth, and out of the undergrowth sprang brambles and hazels, now several years old. However, the space between the four houses and the two raised granaries, which served as the village square, was extremely neat; the grass was short, as if someone came to cut it from time to time. But that was all, because the rest hadn't been touched by human

44

hands in a long time. The rafters of one of the houses had caved in completely and the roof of another was missing tiles and looked like a toothless old man. The gutters had plants growing in them, and only half of those window frames that hadn't been carried off by the wind had any glass in them. A stone stilt that used to prop up one of the raised granaries had collapsed, and the old building knelt on the ground like a vanquished giant or a dying elephant. The last resident had passed away eight years ago, but anyone would think the village had been uninhabited for fifty. Houses, like human hearts, age more in one year when they are empty than they do in twenty with a family inside.

The forest was about to come crashing down over these sandcastles.

A massive cloud like a caravel bound for the Americas, its hold loaded with rain, was sailing slowly across the sky toward him. On earth, night had already fallen, and countless pairs of eyes were watching from behind a thick black curtain of trees. Something landed with a loud thud on the floor of one of the rooms, and he heard the squawk of a crow close by. He sensed that it was one of those nights. The darkness was spreading like India ink, welling up from the ground, imbuing everything with blackness and silence. He didn't have much time.

He pushed the door of the house; it wouldn't open. There was a window on the ground floor, but miraculously it still had all its panes, and he didn't want to break them, not knowing how long he might need to live there. Weeks, months perhaps. He took out the axe. The first blow rang out like a gunshot, something inside the house fled, and a flock of black birds in a nearby tree took flight. On his third attempt, the bolt at the top of the stable door yielded with a crack that echoed through all the rooms, and a current of cold, damp air brushed past him on its way out of the house. Craning his neck as if peering down into a well or the cold, dark earth of a grave, he lit a candle and went inside.

The oldest old woman in the Old World was no longer there, nor was the one-eyed cat, but everything else was the same. In the kitchen, the hearth with its enormous hood that kept the heat in and allowed the entire family to sit underneath, benches pulled up close to the fireside. The walls still just as black, from grease and soot, the hooks still just as rusty and empty. The earth floor had been trodden hard over the years and looked like stone from all the sweeping and scrubbing.

He broke a worm-eaten wooden stool into pieces and crumbled some hulled ears of corn, as dry and shriveled as the old woman's gums. The first spark spread through the air like an aurora borealis, as a myriad of spiders' webs caught alight. Then the kitchen filled with smoke until the stale air inside the flue warmed up and began to circulate again, sucking in the fumes like a grateful smoker. He fetched a moldy foam mattress from one of the bedrooms and placed it on the kitchen floor by the fire. Marcelino fell asleep listening to the crackle of the wood and the patter of the first fat raindrops from the storm on an old corrugated roof.

* * *

When he woke up he felt as though he had been asleep for hours. The fire had gone out and it was not yet day; the dawn chorus hadn't yet begun. He lit a candle and went outside, where he scoured the sky for stars, the moon, or some distant glow that might signal the break of day.

A black cloak enveloped everything and the darkness around him was so thick he could almost touch it. His candle was the only star in the whole sky, on the entire earth.

The night was evil, the night was his mother crying, his brother crying.

His father carried the night in his clenched fist. The night was blood and pain and damp stains on the ceiling shaped like sad faces. The night was freezing sheets and the smell of piss—he would wet himself in sheer terror—and the chatter of teeth and the taste of blood and everything that was bad.

He looked at his hand and arm: his skin was black.

The buzzing sound of a gigantic swarm of angry flies drove him back inside the house. He lit the fire and all the candles he had. Afterward, he lay down and wept, waiting for the darkness to melt into a dark puddle like thick hot chocolate and trickle down through the cracks in the floor.

His father grumbling, cursing, and hurling insults. The foul, hot breath of an alcoholic, his insides rotting away. His big hands, with his stubby fingers stained by the smoke from all the black tobacco he had inhaled on his journey toward an equally black death. His swollen belly and red nose. His father thrashing his idiot son until he saw blood. And then his father moaning in the next room when, having beaten Marcelino, he would climb on top of his mother. His little brother stroking his face, not understanding a thing, and not suspecting that when their father died, the night he carried inside him would find its way into his soul too.

As Marcelino drifted off again, a faint bluish glow began to filter through the windowpanes.

* * *

"And it'll sound like the rustle of the wind in the trees, son. But if you look carefully, you'll see that nothing is moving and that there isn't even the faintest breeze. You'll hear it coming along the road. And though you might understand what it is, and try to avoid it by moving out of its path or going in the opposite direction, it will follow you, slow and inexorable, across time and space, until it catches up with you. You must be a man and accept it.

"You'll keep on walking, toward the sound of creaking wood, and as you turn a corner you'll meet it head-on.

"The first thing you'll notice is the cart moving forward by itself, as if being pulled by invisible horses.

"The second thing is that you'll know the person driving it. But he shouldn't even be there, let alone nodding to you, because he's your neighbor Andrés or Pedro or Juan or whoever, who died last month and whose funeral you attended.

"If you can contain your terror you'll observe the third significant detail: the wheels are made of cork, to help them roll soundlessly over the stones.

"He'll nod as he passes, give you a wide berth, and continue on his path.

"Then, all you can do is wait. It might be tomorrow, or in a month, but it will come. Sooner or later you too will make one final journey, in a cart with cork wheels, to fetch the next person fated to die in your village. It's simple, my son."

* * *

Sometimes one of the seeds carried along by the river comes to rest among the stones at the water's edge and puts down roots. Over a few months the shoot grows healthy and strong, with an abundance of water, no competition, and plentiful sunlight. All spring, summer, and even autumn. But as soon as the snow, the rain, and, most importantly, the thaw arrive, the river level rises by several meters and our friend is invariably swept away.

Is nature wrong? Is it cruel for going to so much trouble, only to put an end to its life in a single stroke?

Nature is indifferent.

There is no life, no death, there is only a vast and never-ending story, a harmony sensed only by fools, artists, and saints.

We have the voice and it is time. We have all time.

* * *

We know it was early November, because the pig had filled out so much it was almost too big for the sty. The best chestnuts in the world grow in those parts, as big as a man's fist, and once the pigs have been fattened up on them they don't survive beyond autumn.

It was a perfect day. A frosty dawn had covered the fields in a blanket of white, as if it had snowed. There was not a single cloud in the crisp cobalt sky, and the air was so dry and pure it stripped the muck from your lungs.

The men were eating fried eggs, chorizo, and potatoes for breakfast, and drinking anis and cider to fire themselves up. The women, with piles of basins of every color at the ready, were dicing huge quantities of onions on great slabs of wood. The pig was grunting nervously inside the pen. They all know when their time is up; they're born for the slaughter, after all. Although sometimes they grunt merely because they're hungry; after weeks of being overfed, they're starved so they shit everything out, leaving their guts clean. The children were playing and shouting and darting about like the swifts that had left the skies a few months back. Lino was one of them. But he wasn't shouting or playing or pestering the grown-ups. He never left his mother's side, just took it all in, wide-eyed. She was a kind soul, who helped the sick, the possessed, the cursed, anyone in need. The father was a bad lot and rough as they come, but he was strong and well versed in slaughter.

At about nine o'clock they brought out the hog, hooked by the neck. It grunted in fear, and people said that it was a fine pig. Together, the men tied its legs with rope so it couldn't move. At Pacho the slaughterman's nod, a woman placed a green basin underneath; it glinted like broken glass on a riverbed.

They worked in silence, save for the pig's shrieks. Pacho took a large old knife, its blade worn thin by a thousand sharpenings, and slit the animal's throat in one stroke. Blood started to gush out, pumped by the pig's frightened heart. Basin after basin filled with blood. A small pool of overflow trickled down the concrete path in rivulets so red and thick they were almost black. The air was heavy with a blend of ozone, joy, excitement, and iron that made you want to laugh and cheer. The blood kept flowing and the women kept stirring to prevent it from coagulating, until there was so much red foam it looked like a demon barber's shaving basin.

Afterward, a man ran a blowtorch over the pig's body to burn off the hair, and others scraped at it with blunt knives to remove any that remained. The blowtorch snorted like a devil.

They raised the hog, tethering it so it stood almost upright, crucified. Pacho heaved the knife into the top of its chest and sliced cleanly downward until the guts fell out pink, purple, gray, and black, and people started clapping like children who have cracked open a piñata. They removed the innards and threw them into various basins. Then they cracked the breastbone with a hatchet and cleaved the chest open. The pig had stopped squealing a while back, but it was still alive; you could see its heart beating in the cold morning air.

Lastly, they hung it head down, a stake holding its chest open to let the air circulate. People began drinking toasts to it. The women got out chairs, trestles, and wooden boards, which they assembled into long tables, covering them with white tablecloths that shone like holy shrouds in the clean autumn light.

They lit a fire in half an old oil drum. Thanks to the liquor and the jovial atmosphere they didn't feel the cold, but while the men carried on in their shirtsleeves, the puddles and trickles of blood had frozen solid. Lino couldn't take his eyes off the pig; thick drips like red paint were falling from its snout. One of the children asked if he wanted to play with them. Lino said nothing and hid his face in his mother's bosom.

The men drank and ate fresh meat, which they roasted on a metal grill on top of the drum. They argued loudly, for fun, like people did back then; and the afternoon drifted into evening.

Casimiro raised his glass: "The body's like a spoiled child, mustn't let 'im get away with it. If 'ee wants water, give 'im wine!" And everyone called out together, "Give 'im wine!"—or "anis!" or "cider!"—and they all laughed merrily. Admittedly, Casimiro was living proof of just how wrong his theory was. His red nose was misshapen and covered in lumps, like a potato. The same lumps covered his huge belly, which hung down almost to his knees and looked more like a sack stuffed with objects of all shapes and sizes than anything else. Indeed, poor old Miro died not long afterward.

And evening became night, and still they kept going. Some began to sing the old songs, the cantos, habaneras, corridos, vaqueiradas, and tonadas; there's nothing quite like a group of friends singing them. The first to break into song was always Culoalhombro. They'd always called him that, on account of the ass-shaped hump on his back, but his voice was as exquisite as his body was deformed, and in the bar they'd always coax him into singing a tonada and he wouldn't hold back. Even now, thirty years since his death, there are old folk who remember him, and on still summer nights they imagine they hear his warm voice floating out from the bar and over the valley.

Culoalhombro would start to sing, and one of the women, usually La Cuca, would accompany him, and gradually other women would join in, and then everyone, and they would sing on and on without a care, one canto after another, while the drinks kept coming; and there were always cigars and they would smoke until the frogs and the birds fell silent, and in those moments you wanted to hug whoever was next to you, even if they were an ass, which they often were, and all was well, and . . . what can we say: this, surely, was true happiness.

* * *

It wasn't that Marcelino's father was a bad drunk, more that he'd always been plain bad. But when he drank too much, he got the Devil inside him. You could almost see that one drink too many going to his head. His eyes would cloud over, turning dull like the river water when a cloud passes in front of the sun. He would stop talking suddenly, even breaking off mid-speech, bow his head, and then, for no apparent reason, take up the same peculiar position: his arm bent and his hand brought up level with his chest. The hand hung loosely from the wrist, almost lifeless. And after that, he would drink and mumble to himself, as if what he saw didn't please him one little bit.

"You're a whore, see. I'm gonna kill you, whore, maybe that'll stop you bringing shame on me." The singing stopped. His hand, still hanging, had clenched itself into a fist, like a scorpion's tail or a snake poised for the kill.

"Oh, come on, man, let's just enjoy the party, for Christ's sake," said Casimiro, who was sitting behind him. "Everyone's having a good time, we're all friends here. Have another drink and let's sing."

"You shut your damn mouth or I'll slit your throat like the swine's," he said, and his hand opened a little, a finger indicating the hung pig. All eyes turned to the pig.

"No one insults me, not even God! So you want to slit my throat? Really? You want to slit my throat? Come on then, motherfucker!" yelled Casimiro, getting to his feet. Some of the others tried to hold him back.

Lino's father didn't move, except for the finger, which retracted into his fist like a snail's head into its shell. His wife moved closer to him. She took him gently by the arm, to let him know it was time to go.

Just then his hand opened, grabbed the knife they'd been using to cut the bread, and sliced Casimiro's hand. Next, he lunged at his wife's throat, the blade nicking her chin before several men threw themselves on him and gripped his arms.

Casimiro didn't stop screaming as the blood poured from his hand, staining the white tablecloth.

Lino's mother said nothing and refused to let anyone tend to her wound. She simply pressed a napkin to her chin, took Lino's hand, excused herself, and left. It was then that

La Cuca noticed she was showing slightly. Fleetingly, she wondered whether she should tell someone, so the woman wouldn't be left to walk home alone. But she didn't, and then she forgot all about it.

* * *

Along came a dog and ate the cat that ate the mouse that ate the cheese that was all the old woman and the old man had to eat.

THE WORMS

The mountainside is all timber forest. At regular intervals, the oldest chestnut trees in one area of forest are felled, leaving the youngest to grow tall and produce new woodland. The whole process takes several decades, and by the time the felling saws reach the last zone, at the top of the mountain, you'd never know the first one had been stripped bare, for the trees look a hundred years old and the animals have forgotten humankind.

Last winter—it's easier to cut the trees in winter when they have no leaves—they began again at the foot of the slopes, and Pando thought it would be the last time he'd see it. He didn't mind. He even felt relieved, as if his own cycle were coming to an end and all humanity were simply an eternal forest where the gods could harvest good timber.

Pando is ninety years old. He's sitting, like he does whenever weather permits, in his chair outside the bar in Carriles, the bar he started as a young lad and that his grandson has now taken over. The customers, mainly local farmworkers who drop in for a glass of wine and a good old grumble, say hello on the way in, and he gives a little nod in reply.

For a long while now he hasn't felt like talking to anyone, only to his memories. And his memories are as boundless as the mountain forest, and every year he remembers more. Last night, for instance, he didn't sleep a wink because in his memory he was walking through the valley exactly as it was more than seventy years ago. Step by step, corner by corner, river bend by river bend, he remembered all the places and people—all dead now—he'd pass when he used to walk from that very bar to the riverbank, by the bridge. He'd even go for a dip, swim up and down a little. He remembered, too, the feel of his cool, young skin drying in the sun.

It's getting dark, but it has been such a gray and cloudy day it feels like dawn when the weakening sun fleetingly breaks through the swollen belly of cloud. The voices of the men talking in the bar are like chickens trying to fly, barely able to flap their wings for a few yards before falling back down and running along the path. Pando watches through the illuminated window as they wave their arms about and gesticulate.

It seems they're all getting quite worked up down there, in San Antolín. Last week there was a girl going around asking questions about Marcelino, and seeing as the girl had spent her summers in the village as a child—she's Marirosa's niece—they were happy to answer them.

Charo told her that Lino's father had been a brute who constantly beat his wife and son, right until his heart, which he never used for anything good, gave out. Fifi told her that Lino's mother was called Olegaria and was born in a poor farmstead up in the mountains, but that she came down when, still a young girl, she married his father, who was more than twenty years her senior. They also claimed that Olegaria had special powers and occasionally practiced witchcraft, but never for money, only to help those in need. It wasn't hard getting out of them that Lino had allegedly been abused by a priest when he was a child, but nothing was ever proved, because Lino had always been a good kid, harmless, but ever so quiet, a bit slow, reserved, keeping himself to himself. Pacho told her that Marcelino's brother, Manuel, was a thug, same as his father. Minín added that he wasn't just a thug, he liked to gamble too, and owed money to half the village. According to Ramón, he left for Madrid when he was very young because he thought he was a cut above the rest and that he'd be one of life's winners, but it turned out that he was a loser at cards and business, and his only talent was for violence and drinking. And, inevitably, a few years ago he'd had to return home, and now he'd gotten himself hooked up with a prostitute he was trying to impress. Between them, they provided Marirosa's niece with a story far more comprehensive than their individual versions, because this was the first time all the strands had been pulled together.

The men are having a discussion in the bar and pointing at the newspaper, which is all creased up, it's been thumbed through that many times: "Bank intended to take Marcelino's house!" the headline on the front-page reads.

It's been years since Pando last read the paper. The news is born, grows up, and dies too quickly for him. He can't take it all in. Like the eucalyptus tree, it doesn't provide decent wood and doesn't allow anything else to grow near it, but the eucalyptus at least is beautiful when it sways in the wind, creaking like the mast of an ancient ship. He rests his rootlike hands on his walking stick. The voices and opinions slip out of the door, disappearing like drunks into the starless night.

* * *

But before we go on, we feel we should clear something up. Only a minute ago, we said that Lino's brother's girlfriend was a prostitute. She was a prostitute, and there's no other way of putting it. The most in-demand prostitute at the Alegrías nightclub, on the outskirts of Villar.

The club is a little two-story house next to an abandoned stretch of the old national road that became obsolete when they built the highway. The façade is blue, with the brick molding on the three front windows painted white. A neon strip light, also blue, extends across the façade, splitting it into two halves. The most striking thing about Alegrías is its powerful skyward-pointing spotlight, installed by the most recent owner, younger and trendier than the previous ones. This spotlight can be seen from several miles away. When it's cloudy, it projects a white circle onto the clouds; when it's misty, a pale beam of light. It has a motor, which changes its position every so often. From a distance, it looks like a lighthouse in the middle of the mountains. A lighthouse to warn you away from the coasts of sadness, and away from the island of the voiceless sirens. It might just be one of the most heartbreaking sights in the entire world, almost as sad as the cheesy music at the empty bumper car ride on a Monday at dusk, or the white neon sign at the shooting gallery on a desolate waste ground when the customers have left, or the cage with the scrawny lion at the tiny little circus under a dirty, faded awning in the Oscos hotel parking lot. Or Enrique's son, once so handsome and clever but now driven mad by reading too many books, walking along the riverside, hand in hand with his grandmother like a little boy, saliva dribbling from the corner of his lips, his once-shining eyes now almost hidden in a face all swollen and fat from medication.

She was better off here than in her hometown in the Dominican Republic, she was sure of that; Sabana Yegua was a hot, mosquito-ridden shithole in the jungle. Here, she was queen for the simple fact that she came from there. She used to hope that one day her boyfriend would take her away from all this, but in truth it seemed it was she who was helping him escape from himself. Maybe she didn't actually love him, but he would make her head spin with all the things he promised her, and she always fell for his lies. Now he couldn't fool her anymore. No. She was still young, next time she'd choose more wisely.

She's no different than anyone else. She wants a house and not to have to work; some money and to be looked after. The men are ugly and a bit rough, but generally harmless, and they do have money, and all they want is for their women to be nice to them, make them food, and wash their clothes, and they don't expect a girl to fall in love with them, just care for them a little and not sleep with other men. She's no different than anyone else. If Lena, the Russian, could get Nachón, who's not only a veterinarian but a decent man to boot, why shouldn't she? If Princila, the Cuban, could snap up that guy from Piensos Cabruñana, who treats her like a princess, why shouldn't she? If Macarira, who's practically from next door, from Sabana Plana, could marry Andrés the truck driver, so can she. She simply has to watch out and not allow herself to be taken in by the first guy with a tie and a pretty smile who orders a bottle of cheap champagne. She's still young, and someday her brave farmer will come, sweep her onto his shining tractor, and carry her off to his castle. But what should she do with all the promises now, where should she keep all the words, which makeup remover should she use to wipe off her smile without harming her skin, which perfume should she apply to mask the whiff of widow that scares everyone away? Perhaps she should move on again. She might find more suitable castaways on a different island. For now, though, let's leave her there, propped up at the bar; she's used up the three days she allowed herself to mourn.

* * *

Like all children, Lino was reborn with every new day. And the new day came, bringing with it the light that chased away his fears. We can't tell you what he did that first day. In fact, we don't know for sure what he did for any of that week he spent in the old house. Like all trees, Lino makes no sound when he falls in the forest, unless we're there to tell the story. But we don't need to see him fall to spot a rotten trunk, or broken branches, or at least a hole, a gap in the forest, some trace of him. And so we do know that he used his new axe to chop up, among many other things, a worm-eaten dresser, a rickety old table, and a section of wooden flooring that had fallen through the collapsed ceiling. Too much wood, actually, as if he was naively planning to stay a few months. Although it must also have been to keep busy, because the Reverend Father had taught him that the Devil makes work for idle hands. He hacked back some of the undergrowth too, and cut a concealed path through the thicket, like the ones animals use to get down to the river to drink. Marcelino went into the other houses and gathered up anything that might be useful: a broken sickle, two brass knives left over from a piti-ful long-lost cutlery set, a plastic bucket, a stool. And most importantly, in a drawer in the house where he was living, he found two black-and-white photos almost completely faded by the years. In one, you could just about see a girl with long plaits, wooden clogs, and an apron, standing beside a large cow with a yoke. Her face is a blur of light in which you can make out two points where her eyes should be. The other was a group photo. Thirty people are gathered around a bagpiper and a ram with big curly horns. Almost all of them are chil-dren. The ram is doubtless a raffle prize from a fiesta in some village or other, and the field has been turned into a swamp by days' worth of rain and getting trampled by revelers at the *romería* celebrations; many of the children are caked in mud up to their knees. You can't pick out the faces in this photo either, but a penciled cross marks out one child—one of the few not wearing a beret—from all the others. For Marcelino, this alone made the long journey worthwhile, because he knew straight away that both the girl with plaits and the girl marked with a cross were none other than his mother. He wrapped the photographs in a handkerchief and put them in the metal box along with his other treasures.

That is all we know. But it certainly gave him time to think. He'd never been so idle. His whole life, right from when he learned to walk, had been nothing but working and striving, first on his father's orders, then to feed his brother, and lastly for himself, and because he didn't know any other way.

Milking, mowing, feeding, peeling, cutting, felling, chopping, repairing, distributing, grafting, harvesting, sowing, struggling, germinating, pruning, crushing, expressing, bottling, corking, preserving, ploughing, plastering, aerating, drying, stacking, castrating, breeding, plucking, gutting, bleeding, chorizo-making, drying, desiccating, curing, shredding, storing, burying, packing, salting, pickling, pressing, burning, digging, killing, calf-delivering, throwing, climbing, knocking down, drilling, retiling, sawing, working, working, working.

The Devil makes work for idle hands. If that's true, the Devil was in luck. Much as Marcelino wanted to be busy, he had no choice but to watch and wait. To let the thoughts come, take a furtive look around and leave again. To try not to let the memories bite, because everyone knows memories are like Dobermans, and the older they get, the more likely they are to turn on their owners. For now, Marcelino's thought process is like that of a child learning to spell. A retired builder on a construction site, with nothing to build. A sailor, seasick on land. A pair of bowlegs, deformed by too much riding.

* * *

"All trees are in love with the Sun, my love, but the Oak is the one who loves her the most. And so the Oak grew his branches for hundreds of years, to reach high enough to embrace her. The Sun, who was in love with the Oak too, put out her fire, so as not to burn him.

"Out of this embrace sprung the Night.

"But the Sun and the Oak were locked in their embrace for so long that it grew cold and the vermin crept out from the shadows and took over the earth, the grain we turn into bread began to rot, the apple blossoms didn't become apples, and the grass lay down to sleep, awaiting death.

"Thankfully, the Sun became pregnant, and after twenty-eight days gave birth to the Moon, who scared away the vermin and lit the way for those who were lost.

"The Oak wanted to caress his beautiful daughter, so he stopped embracing the Sun and reached out a branch to touch his daughter's white face. The Sun felt insulted and betrayed and was so envious of the Moon's serene beauty that she burned with all her might to scare her, accidentally burning the Oak's branches. Now a very old tree, he could no longer grow his branches high enough. Ever since then, he simply gazes on the Sun and Moon with sadness and longing.

"The Sun is very proud and blames the Moon for her misfortune: every day, she burns so fiercely that nobody can admire the Moon's beauty. But she burns so ferociously that she exhausts herself and falls asleep. And only then does the Moon dare to venture out from her hiding place behind the hills and smile at her father."

* * *

The Vaqueiros live in the mountains in eastern Asturias and are known for their unique folklore and customs. These families, cattle farmers since ancient times, head to the highest mountain passes with their herds at the first sign of warm weather and live there until the cold and snow force them to decamp to the lower slopes on the coast. Interestingly, they have hardly ever interbred with other ethnic groups, and most of them are therefore red-haired, with pale freckly skin. They are shunned by almost everyone, including the locals, who at some point branded them all crazy.

There is a Vaqueiro song that goes like this:

> *Reverend Father doesn't dance*
> *Lest his crown should fall*
> *Dance, dance, Reverend Father*
> *God shall pardon all.*

It's the only song Lino managed to learn in his entire life; it made him happy but hurt him even more, both at once.

He liked seeing his mother at the *romería* festival in San Antolín, smiling, wearing her pretty flowered dress—instead of the dirty black apron she wore every day—tambourine in hand, singing in the nasal, primitive, atonal, ancestral voice that the song demands, like the spirits sing it, with all the other women. They would all be sitting on a large red-and-white checked rug laid out on the field by the church. The church was small and squat, just a square floor with thick stone walls, built centuries earlier by the ancestors of the very people who were celebrating San Antonio now. Lino liked the church too. And the people, when they were simply having fun and not trying to convince him of anything. And the other children, running, jumping, throwing stones, making a racket, with their skin and pristine clothes as unadulterated as their joy.

"Where are you off to, you little rascal, come back here, don't get your trousers dirty."

"It's always such lovely weather for San Antolín."

The bitter smell of spilled cider on the freshly mown grass. The night, when it was a fine night, with millions of crickets also singing: "You just put a twig in the little hole, the silly thing clings on and you've got him."

All the constellations. The ones up there, suspended in their glass of spilled milk, with their heavenly bodies and planets, the same ones from which, in front of our eyes, stars fell and turned into fireflies gleaming in the grass. And the one down here, made from hundreds of brightly colored bulbs hanging from a tall wooden post that had been heaved into position by the village lads, so strong, so mighty, capable of moving mountains, and so proud of their efforts, which were trivial, perhaps, but also indispensable.

"It's getting chilly."

The women rubbing their bare arms, which shone delicately as if they'd never been sunburned from working in the fields, before putting on their little cardigans and resting their heads on the shoulders of the men who loved them, or who they wanted to love them, like a falling leaf settles on a moss-covered stone. The firecrackers bought at a stall belonging to a tiny thousand-year-old lady, no more than a bag of bones covered with skin so wrinkled and leathery she might have been a wicked witch. And she might have been, if it weren't for her small moist eyes glistening like black pebbles on a riverbed, smiling kindly at the children as she served them.

Just this. And bagpipers, and a bar made from wooden planks on top of trestles, where the oldest would drink and the youngest would drink, and sometimes they'd fight each other with good, clean punches to show how manly they were. Just this, nothing special, a nothing repeated in so many insignificant valleys across so many centuries by so many men and women, in so many riverbeds, carried along by so much long-forgotten history. Just this was undoubtedly the most perfect thing in the universe. The song made him happy.

* * *

But the words to the song didn't make him happy, and this was precisely why he remembered them. The stubbornness of pain; the more you try to wriggle free from its rusty hook, the deeper it sinks into your flesh. The Reverend Father was dancing. The Reverend Father couldn't care less about the Lord God's forgiveness.

"Dance, Marcelino. I will forgive you."

God certainly wasn't present in the plaster statues that filled the little church with their brittle gesturing arms, their bleeding wounds, their disapproval. Nor in the shabby confessional, dulled by countless fidgeting hands, consumed by the woodworm of shame and whispered sins. Nor was He present in the vaulted ceiling, never adorned by any artist. Nor in the prayer kneelers or the pews where people would beg forgiveness for simply being human. Nor in the silver cup of spilled blood. Nor in the unleavened white bread. Nor in the candles for San Antonio, which would flicker, in danger of being blown out by the vigorous draught of unfulfilled dreams. Perhaps He was present in the church bell that rang out across the valley at nightfall or announced that someone had died but that everything remained beautiful all the same. Perhaps in the cold stone, against which Lino pressed his face after each blow the Reverend Father dealt him when he cried or complained. In that stone, in that stone's ever-steady nerves, in the sound of the stone's beating heart to which saints and fools alone can listen without fear of being struck down. Maybe in the magnificent old yew tree planted on a grave over seven hundred years ago, next to which the church was built. The tree where, until very recently, murderers used to be executed, and beneath which grew the mandrake after the earth had been showered with the hanged men's semen in their dying spasms. Maybe He was in the lime they used to paint the stone walls every year. Maybe in the rattle of a coin dropped discreetly onto the collection plate by an old lady for those supposedly more in need of charity than she. Maybe. Surely. But certainly not in the black cassock; nor in the weak, pale, mortal body it concealed.

"You're wicked, Marcelino. Dance, and let us pray that God will forgive you.

"Put this in your mouth and suck and let us pray you'll get to heaven.

"Take your trousers off. That's it, now bend over the table. You know if you tell a soul you'll go to Hell. This must be our secret."

> Reverend Father doesn't dance
> Lest his crown should fall
> Dance, dance, Reverend Father
> God shall pardon all.

This song made him happy. No, he hated it.

* * *

When you see a weed in the vegetable plot, you pull it out. When you've got more chickens than you need, you wring the neck of one and chuck it in the pot. When some dog mounts your bitch and she gives birth to a litter, you choose the best puppy, put the rest in an old potato sack with some stones, and throw the sack in the river. When an apple tree no longer bears fruit, you cut it down and chop it up for firewood. When the grass in your field gets too long, you cut it, gather it up, and store it in the hayloft. When a man in a suit comes and shows you some papers and tells you some stuff about mortgages and wants to take away your vegetable plot, your hens, your bitch, and your fields, you defend yourself. Even if this man in a suit is your brother. And they can call you a revolutionary and talk about you on TV and in the papers and say who knows what about the oppressed peoples, or the last remaining guerrilla, but the truth is simpler, it's always simpler. And the truth is that you have to do what you have to do. None of the rest matters, not one bit; after the winter comes another winter, after you cut the grass, you must cut it again, after the harvest, you must harvest countless more times, this year's snowfall will thaw and another will come in its place, this body will rot and other bodies will tread in its footsteps. You see, this wound hurts just as much as yesterday's wound, which hurt as much as the one before, and the one before the one before that, and as much as the first wound, the original wound that the first man feared. And though this wound is bleeding in the same way as all wounds bleed, and blood has always been the same, this wound thinks itself unique.

* * *

They were making so much noise you'd have thought they were trying to alert every living creature within a half-mile radius to their presence. They were probably even more scared than the fugitive and hoping that whatever was inside those houses—animal, ghost, or a simpleton with a gun— would make a run for it. The thing was, they were mostly local police who'd only ever had to get their pistols out to clean them and who obviously weren't used to hunting people down, as they knew everyone; the real switchboard was the bar in their local watering hole after they'd finished their shift. If they hadn't been making such a racket, they'd have caught Marcelino no problem, given that he was sound asleep when they showed up. In fact, they were so clueless that they didn't even spot the plume of smoke rising from the chimney of the house where Marcelino was sleeping and instead headed straight for the house with the huge holes in the roof, breaking the door down with such a bang that they woke not only Marcelino, but all the animals in the forest.

And so it was that three minutes later Marcelino had already slipped out of the back window and, making use of the path he'd cut through the undergrowth, gotten away unseen, hiding himself behind some large rocks, themselves grown over by hazel trees. He tried to stay awake, but it was a dark night, he could barely see, and eventually tiredness got the better of him.

Marcelino awoke at that indeterminate hour when the day turns a new page before a new one has been written. He checked his belongings and realized that, in his haste, he'd forgotten his new axe. He retraced his steps cautiously.

He couldn't see his brother, but there were five men dressed in green in front of the house. Several of them were smoking, and the smoke rose unimpeded into the crisp morning air. They seemed nervous, all turning their heads at the slightest sound—a bird or a falling leaf. Thankfully, Marcelino was less inclined to show off than a bird and had more to lose than a dried-up leaf, so he watched from the trees without giving himself away. One of the men spoke on the telephone, and another gave an order to a third, who disappeared and came back a short while later with Marcelino's axe. They stood looking at it. The red tip, the blade shining like silver.

* * *

There are few places more authentic, more full of life, than an ironmonger's on market day, when they put their most impressive farm equipment on show to tempt the locals who've come down from the small villages in clean shirts, ready cash in their pockets. The woven hazel baskets that more and more tourists are snapping up to place by the hearth in their holiday cottages; the sickles, the spades, and the scythes, newly fashioned from metal that glistens as if it's wet, sharp blades eager to cut cleanly through fresh grass; the pitchforks, the mattocks, and the wooden rakes, newly sanded and almost white but which, over time, will develop a dark patina from the rain and frequent handling; brooms of the kind once ridden by witches; the pungent leather saddles and the yokes like plump grotesque cushions; boxes full of young plants—kale, lettuce, tomato, and pumpkins— that are all bursting with new hope and sell by the dozen. Everyone, even the most die-hard urbanite, feels safe here. If modern civilization collapsed, you'd have everything needed to rebuild a country.

This is why Artemio is so sparing with his words. He knows his mission, and he knows it is a just mission. If people want to chat, there's the bar. If they come to his ironmonger's, they should come with clear ideas or well-thought-out questions. The customers know this, and they're not surprised when he doesn't even meet their gaze as he weighs out the nails that tinkle sublimely on the old scales, or when he opens and closes the cash register with an abrupt mechanical gesture or greets them with a simple quiet grunt and doesn't say goodbye. This is normal for him. He is the chief tool of all the tools. But the truth is that today he's in a reflective mood.

In the early hours, he read that Marcelino had narrowly escaped from the local police. He read standing up, like he did every morning, leaning against his ancient wooden worktop—"If it ain't broke, don't fix it," as they used to say in the Old World. They were explaining that, all this time, Marcelino had been hiding in Cuanxú, the miserable little farmstead where his mother was born. Poor devil, he thought. They were suggesting that the police had found enough evidence in one of the houses to indicate that Marcelino had spent several nights there: a still-warm fire, food scraps, and the axe Marcelino had picked up in San Antolín last time he was here. They were saying that the net was closing in, and it wouldn't be long before they found him. Probably for the best, he told himself, and then the doorbell rang and he closed the paper.

But he couldn't stop thinking about it all day. Specifically, he couldn't get it out of his head that Marcelino had lost his new axe. In Artemio's mind, nothing was as terrible as this—not the fratricide, the hunger, the persecution, or the cold, and not even the hype that was building up around the poor fool. The nail is for nailing, the saw blade is for sawing, and perhaps what they were saying about Marcelino was true and it was his role in life to represent the oppressed: if that was his function, then so be it. But for some reason, the fate of the axe, a tool that would never be used, seemed to him particularly cruel.

He would never have sold it if he'd known.

* * *

They scoured the hills, but they didn't find his hiding place. The Rambo of Cobre, the alleged assassin, the fugitive from the North, the Asturian Cain, Silly Billy the Kid, the autistic Robin Hood, the abused fool, the bullied turned bully, the outraged outcast, the original victim, your favorite country bumpkin, armed and dangerous, a twenty-first-century Spanish Maqui, he who is all of us and who goes by a whole host of names, now almost never just Marcelino or Lino—he had hidden in an old iron mine.

The entrance to the mine had collapsed years earlier, and now the only way in was to squeeze through a small opening and crawl for several yards. This passage opened out into a surprisingly spacious chamber. The walls, a mixture of clay and iron ore, were covered in paintings and graffiti, no doubt from a time when the mine was more accessible: from hearts drawn by local couples who'd gone there to make love, to simple names and dates written by bored young lads, to paintings from the war, during which it had first been a hideout and then a makeshift prison. They had all obeyed the same unconscious impulse as the first man to leave his handprints on the walls of his cave for posterity. That first message, that "I am human," that "here I am and I'm here to stay." The large chamber led to a narrower gallery which tunnelled deep into the ground, and from down there came a whispering sound. It wasn't the dwarves that everyone knows live in mines, but the stream that the first miners had diverted so that they could break through the mountain and separate the earth from the mineral deposits.

He didn't have much food left, as the bread and cookies had gone moldy. The fire didn't really illuminate the chamber; the red walls soaked up the light like a sponge. It didn't create much warmth either, because the cave was as cold and damp as a pot on an unlit stove. But he stayed hidden there for four days. He was so scared of his brother and his friends. No one knows what he did or thought for all that time. One thing was for sure: he didn't add his name to the graffiti on the walls.

When he finally emerged, dragging his body out of the hole, he was caked in mud and had to close his eyes in the dazzlingly bright daylight: if anyone had seen him they would have feared the earth had spawned a new demon.

* * *

Thankfully, there are always women. Men chain-smoke nervously, secretly irritated by the waiting and the whole time-consuming process. Men don't want the ending to drag on, they want it all to be over with and the corpse buried as soon as possible so that they can bravely face up to the wreckage and go back to hunting mammoths and smearing their bodies with fresh blood, and rebuild the foundations of their new houses, which this time will be solid, will withstand anything. Men learn as egoists learn. When they suffer, it's because they think they could have avoided it.

But there are always women, resisting, holding on, slowly chewing over their grief, bidding farewell to the dying, watching over the dead, dressing even the biggest coward in his hero's shroud. Because a woman watches over a dying man knowing, like all women, that the real miracle is the giving of life, and so understands that it should end simply, without any fuss.

Death is never heroic. Life can be, but not death. Death comes to us all, but we know that if a woman watches over us on our deathbed, we'll go to heaven.

Woman does not weep for the warrior; she weeps for the child who was born and who always leaves this world too soon.

* * *

And so in the tiny chapel of rest, a sterile room with dark scuff marks on the walls from the backs of the plastic chairs lined up along the sides, it was the women who sat watching over Marcelino's brother's body. The men, on the other hand, simply offered their condolences to the girlfriend and headed straight to the funeral parlor's bar.

All the same, everyone was feeling slightly nervous that day. It wasn't a normal funeral. How could it be? Crowds of journalists and cameramen who weren't allowed to enter were waiting outside, pestering people with questions they couldn't have answered even if they'd wanted to. What's more, the murderer was still on the loose, hiding not far away in the forest.

* * *

All the dead are good. There's no use in holding a grudge against a dead person. What's more, if you're angry with a dead person, it means admitting that they might be angry with you, and nobody, absolutely nobody, wants that.

And the dead are good because they are the final mark, the last page of a novel we can finally put down. They are both an ending and a new beginning in our lives; they stay behind and allow us to carry on.

All the dead are good because they're no longer alive and can therefore be imagined. As with fools and saints, we can lie about them because they can't defend themselves. They are a tale with countless morals, an illustration of whatever you like, a myth to be molded. The dead don't belong to the dead; the dead are ours.

* * *

Many people were wracking their brains trying to recall if they'd ever offended Lino, afraid he might have his revenge on all of them. And the deeper they dug, the more they found. Fear is a great archaeologist.

Pacho, for example, remembered one evening in the bar when they were young. He was a bit drunk. He offered to take Lino to visit some prostitutes, and Lino replied that he wasn't interested. So Pacho asked if he'd prefer cows. To which Lino said that of course cows were better: they were nice, provided meat and milk, and didn't bother anyone. So

Pacho, speaking in a loud voice so everyone could hear, said that Lino's child would have horns and a tail like its mother, which was greeted with howls of laughter and a stream of jokes in the same vein. He also remembered that on that same night, blind drunk, they'd sneaked into the poor fool's cowshed, put a cloth like a bride's veil on one of his cows, taken her out into the street, and woken him up by throwing stones at his window, singing: "It's Lino's wedding, oh what fun, I'll fetch my cows and give him one!"

* * *

Big Miguel, Paco, José, and countless others who were boys and young lads around the same time as Lino also recalled with growing unease the days when they'd called him simple and queer, back when the rumor went around that he'd been up to no good with the priest.

"But . . ."

"No, I never did anything to him, and God knows I always tried to stamp out the rumors."

"His brother was a bastard, a thug, I never liked him, *and* he still owes me money."

"I always felt sorry for the poor boy."

"I always said we should help him."

"Obviously . . ."

"Just as well . . ."

"The thing is . . ."

And they genuinely didn't feel they'd treated him badly, and the truth is, they hadn't. They'd pretty much left him to his own devices, like he'd wanted. When they grew up they simply left him in peace. They didn't try to save him or to integrate him into a society in which he clearly didn't fit.

They hadn't even thought about him for years, at least no more than you would about a friendly stray dog you wouldn't want near your children but wouldn't bother chasing off either.

And Marcelino was good; and the dead person, on this occasion, was bad.

"All the dead are bad, and this one's the worst of all; and if I hadn't known his mother, I wouldn't even have turned up to offer my condolences to that whore of his."

No one was to blame, and they would do everything in their power to help Marcelino.

* * *

Along came a stick and killed the dog that ate the cat that ate the mouse that ate the cheese that was all the old woman and the old man had to eat.

* * *

Although possibly of all his troubles the thing that upset him the most was that the moisture in the cave had made the cookies go soft. As we've already mentioned, these cheap cookies were his only luxury in an otherwise extremely frugal diet. They were the same cookies Olvido used to give him.

* * *

Olvido was an elderly seamstress who lived in a little single-story house built on land that belonged to nobody, like many workers' cottages, on the river embankment just before the bridge.

Day after day, from her stool by the fireside, she would peer out through her little kitchen window at the same stretch of dirt track and chat with any neighbors who happened to be passing. When Olvido was a girl a severe polio infection had left her lame, and she'd never in her entire life ventured out of the valley or seen the sea. She could barely write her own name. She'd never had children or a husband, but she loved all the world's children. Every month she would buy them a packet of María Fontaneda cookies, which she would share out among the ones who came to visit.

The children would appear running and shrieking like a flock of birds, and Olvido's face would light up with happiness. They all loved her very much and smothered her with hugs and kisses, even though she was ugly and hunchbacked and had black warts on her face like a witch. She also loved and gave cookies to the children who came alone, like Lino when he stopped by on his way down to town with his mother. Despite receiving only a modest pension, and being obliged to carry on mending clothes to afford the chorizo she liked in her daily bowl of cabbage stew, she unstintingly dished out endless flour-and-egg coins.

But few people visited during the last years of her life. The dirt track was paved and became a main road. All the cars and the crazy speeds they drove at meant that hardly anyone walked past her tiny window, or smiled at her through it, or called out a friendly greeting. The shoals of children she could fish from were dwindling, what with television, video games, and extracurricular activities. And processed sweets

and indulgent parents meant that children no longer appreciated the value of a cookie given with love. Nevertheless, the
odd child would still occasionally drop by of an afternoon,
sent by their mother, or because they were bored, or out of
pure kindness, and then she would reawaken like a flower in
the morning. She would shower the child with kisses, give
them a ton of cookies which she'd kept for so long that they'd
gone stale, and, after making them promise they'd come again
soon, send them off with their hoard of gold coins. Anyone
coming along the road and looking through the window
would have seen her smiling face, reliving the last visit, like
someone warming their hands on a little flame. Not far from
her house, on the other side of the river, there was a small
garbage heap, well known to the local pigeons. It was here
that these latest children dumped the cookies they'd accepted
to make her happy.

One day, Benjamina went to visit her and they had a
long chat. At some point in the conversation, after listening to her talk about this or that child, Benjamina asked her
why she'd never had children herself, seeing as she liked them
so much.

"Ah, there's nothing I'd have loved more. I even had a lad
who loved me and wanted to marry me," Olvido explained.
"I know I'm ugly, but at least I'm not ugly and wicked."

"So what happened?" asked Benjamina.

"What do you think? I had to leave him because he'd
have wanted children. And that was never going to happen."

"I don't understand you, woman. Why ever not?"

"Because I care too much about the little mites to bring one into the world cursed with this," she explained, extending her deformed leg, which was twisted and shorter than the other.

It was then that Benjamina understood and nodded. She left without telling Olvido that the polio that had crippled her as a baby wasn't a hereditary illness, it was a virus, and so she could have had all the children in the world. She thought that Olvido didn't need to know now.

Marcelino continued to drop by to say hello every time he went down to the village, even as an adult, and she still gave him cookies because she said he was her favorite little boy, until the day came when she had need of all those coins to pay the ferryman for her crossing.

* * *

The only truth is a story that is continuously written and rewritten. We drag the truth around with us, oblivious, just as a comet is unaware of its tail. A story we've been telling for so long, and which we hope to carry on telling to our grandchildren.

And in this story everything is of equal importance, and at the precise moment that Hitler was firing a bullet into his temple, Francisco the curate was holding between his fingers a small green bud on a tree branch, a sign that after an especially hard winter, spring had finally arrived. As Ramón Mercader was bashing in Trotsky's brains with an ice pick, Ramona la Cachín was embracing the husband she hadn't seen for years, a poor soldier so shortsighted he didn't manage to fire a single shot in the entire Civil War. As Lenin was crossing the Finnish-Russian border by train en route to St. Petersburg, where the revolution had just begun, while he was gazing out of the window at the infinite snowy landscape, five-year-old Juanín was standing outside his house enjoying his first snowfall, sticking out his tongue to catch the snow-flakes, surprised they didn't taste sweet like he'd imagined. Pepín was calling out something flirtatious to Ana, who was returning from the wash house with a pile of white sheets that she would hang out under the fig tree to brighten in the sun, and Marigel, who was looking at him disapprovingly, sniffed the air, worried that her stew was burning. Joaquín was walk-ing along the road with his hands in his trouser pockets and nodding to Manolo, who was riding by, smiling and show-ing off his new motorbike, and Angustias was watching the leaves being swept along the path by the wind and thinking how quickly autumn had arrived, at the precise moment the Russian leader Nikita Khrushchev was swilling his glass of vodka, rubbing his temples, and fleetingly imagining himself launching a bunch of nuclear missiles at the United States once and for all. And all of Kennedy's headaches disappeared in one fell swoop at the same time as Ramón de Miranda came into the world, not that Ramón was the American rein-carnate. And Juanín was looking out from his living room window at the freshly cut grass in the field while he drank a cup of milky coffee, and Marora was having an orgasm, and Sara was confessing to the priest, and Olegaria, Marcelino's mother, was resting her hand, gentle as a bird, on her tired son's shoulder, at the precise moment the first plane plowed into the Twin Towers.

Everything is happening at this moment and it's all of equal importance, the only difference being who is telling the story and why. Everything is a miracle.

We have the voice, we have the time, we have all time.

This is the moment.

* * *

The first to arrive were two lads who set up camp in La Mouta field, beside the river. Two days later, some of their friends turned up. Casimiro, who owned the field, didn't complain and let them stay. They weren't doing any harm. They lit campfires at night and drank and laughed. A few local boys went down to join the party. Some videos were posted online and then kids began to arrive from all over, some by car, bus, or train, others hitchhiking or on foot.

Pando can hear their laughter close by; he's sitting at one of the plastic tables his grandson brought from the storeroom to seat more customers outside. At the bottom of the valley, he can see the large campsite hugging the banks of the river, and from it he can hear a muffled roar, half drowned-out cries, and the beating of drums. A delivery man is making such a din unloading the countless crates of cider that anyone would think he was doing it on purpose. They'll get through them all, his grandson is smart, which is why Pando leaves the business side to him—the kids at the next table alone have put away six bottles and are still ordering. The lifelong regulars aren't playing cards today either: they're enjoying watching and criticizing the kids, and the kids are enjoying themselves all the more knowing that they have an audience.

Somebody asked them straight out: "So why the hell are you lot here protesting for someone who doesn't have a bloody clue what protesting even is?"

"We're doing it for the village idiot," they replied mischievously. But now the locals are tired of these answers, which sound hollow to them, like TV ads. They can't imagine how fighting for something could be fun, and these kids are having a great time.

Pando is still sitting there, legs slightly apart, checked slippers on his feet, hands resting on the walking stick between his knees, staring straight ahead as if lost in his thoughts. But he knows they're there, and he hears their surprised laughter when they spot him sitting by the door. They try to imagine the life the old man must have led, and they can't. They're still at the beginning of their lives and peering into the ending makes them feel dizzy. They believe that a person's life only counts if it's chock-full of experiences, as if the value of a life can be measured. Most of them feel a mixture of pity and admiration for this stony-faced old man, as if they were contemplating a temple built by the followers of some strange religion that might somehow be their own. They would like to ask him something, but first they'll have to learn how to question.

* * *

A girl takes a selfie with Pando in the background, as if he were sitting on her shoulder.

Gradually night begins to fall, and the laughter continues. The outside light, which hasn't been used for years, is turned on. In the bar, some men even start to sing. Sometimes they don't quite know all the words and lower their voices while they try to work it out, and then raise them again triumphantly. Pando feels like he is inside one of his loveliest memories, when the evenings lasted forever and everyone was young.

* * *

"And the River fell in love with the Moon, and at night he would command all the creatures in his realm to remain silent, while he gazed at her and murmured seductively.

"But the Moon never noticed him.

"And so the River became a furious torrent to impress her. But she remained oblivious to him. And so the River transformed himself into a gentle stream. But she paid him no attention. And so the River transformed himself into a thunderous waterfall. Still nothing. And so the River tried freezing himself to look like a diamond. But the Moon had no interest in jewels and didn't so much as look at him. Finally, in desperation and tired of flowing in vain, he transformed himself into a tranquil mountain lake.

"It was then that the Moon, seeing herself reflected in him and dazzled by her own beauty, embraced him. But the River could not help but extinguish her light with his water and she fled, frightened and cold. As she is pure and has no memory, though, the Moon recovered from the shock and again shone brightly, caught sight of her own reflection, and tried to embrace him. It would always end with her extinguishing her own light and fleeing, but the River was happy in these fleeting moments, and such was his desire to relive them that, since then, all the waters of the world have risen up, longing for the Moon's embrace."

* * *

The flies were buzzing and diving in suicidal spirals, as if tracing the letters of some demented script in the air, and the ancient acrid smell of excrement seemed more pungent than ever.

The hens—trying to escape the clutches of the young village boys who chased them around, laughing and cursing in equal measure—were clucking and flapping in fear, running in desperate circles, taking off just inches before crashing into the walls; it didn't even occur to them to go through the small gap that would have taken them out into the yard. The air they kicked up behind them was full of dust and feathers, which sparkled in the light streaming in through the small window that had been fixed shut with rusty wire. "Fucking help us then, man!" they shouted at the third boy, Lino, who didn't respond.

Eventually, they managed to catch one, grabbing it roughly by the neck. As soon as the chasing stopped, the other hens calmed down, forgot the terror of a few seconds earlier, and carried on clucking and pecking at crumbs that only they could spot amid all the excrement covering the ground.

The boys smiled with satisfaction and one of them held the hen's head in an armlock. "Look, Lino," he said, pushing a finger into the vagina of the uncomplaining bird. "Ah, it's like a woman's cunt . . . "

"Let me try, man!" said the other one, and put his finger in too. "Yeah, it really is."

"Your turn, Lino," he said. Lino hesitated. "Put your fucking finger in!" the boy ordered.

And Lino did as he was told.

Once his finger was inside, it felt much more spacious and warm than he had expected. The hen appeared indifferent to the intruding finger, despite the fact that the orifice was reacting to his movements and squeezing the base of his finger tightly. As if the uterus were independent of the bird. Or as if its reproductive organs were the only important part, the real live being, and the chicken simply a chattel, an add-on, an appendage of the great uterus. Suddenly he felt something throb, and a strong contraction enveloped his whole finger, making him pull it out in fear. The two boys burst out laughing.

"It doesn't bite, you idiot," said the one holding her. "Let's see, you take her. Let's give her some of this."

He pulled down his trousers to reveal an erect penis. As he inserted it he groaned. It didn't take long, merely a few seconds.

Afterward it was the other one's turn. Lino felt slightly sick as he watched all this, as if he were riding on a cart along a road littered with potholes.

"That's good, oh yes, that's good," the other one whispered, and took hold of the hen himself. He was shrieking and writing. Finally, he held his breath and then exhaled slowly. His legs were trembling slightly.

The first one fell about laughing at his friend, still not quite with it, with the hen dangling from his penis, its neck broken and its head hanging lifelessly. His friend let the dead bird drop to the floor.

"You're an animal! At least it was only a chicken, not a woman. Beast!" cried the first one, as if his friend had pulled off some great feat.

"What do you want me to say? Once I get going, there's no stopping me."

When they had calmed down, they looked at Lino, who hadn't said a word.

"Aw, Lino, you're still a virgin."

Lino didn't answer. The Beast picked up the hen and handed it to him.

"Go on, take it, I can't keep it. I won't tell my father. He'll think it was the fox. But not a word, eh? Our little secret. Tell your mother we found it lying in an alley."

"Hey, you've missed out on a lay, but you've got a nice tasty chicken for dinner," said the other one.

"Yeah, man! And it's ready stuffed!" And the two of them laughed.

But they were wrong, because as soon as Lino got home, he threw the chicken to the pigs, who devoured it, feathers and all. They were also wrong in thinking there'd be other chances for Marcelino, because from that day on he didn't even masturbate like everyone else his age, and he never set foot in the brothel that, as soon as they'd outgrown chickens, the others started to frequent in search of the same.

The Devil had been inside there too. Lino had felt him catch hold of his finger and try to draw him in.

* * *

The old roads, the good ones, which are humankind's rivers stamped into the earth by thousands, hundreds of thousands of feet over the centuries, are also disappearing. Before long, there will be nothing but highways connecting the big cities to one another, and the rest of the world will be a rubbish dump or a forest where no one goes. Motorways are gigantic, ridiculous arteries that transport too much blood toward a few shriveled-up, greedy, and ineffectual organs; cities are nothing but enormous blood clots.

With the old roads, on the other hand, we used to spread ourselves out evenly across maps; we didn't feel this need to defile everything that could be defiled. We had no choice but to either get bored or find ways to entertain ourselves without enslaved peoples or countries prostituting themselves so that we could have a good time. With the old roads, the world was big enough. Even if you went by cart or on horseback, it would take you half a lifetime to travel around the world, a fair price to pay for such an adventure. What's more, with the old roads it was possible to go, to get away, and even come back having really gone somewhere. But the old roads, like the individual stories on which the universe was built, are disappearing.

Yes, the old roads are disappearing. It isn't surprising, then, that Marcelino spent the following week sleeping in a car that had been abandoned decades earlier next to a brook and which was now no more than a rusty shell with a back seat. You might not expect to find such a thing in the wilderness, but it's not that uncommon; back then, breakers' yards were few and far between, and a car takes longer to completely disappear than one of the old roads, which are quickly overrun by vegetation. Having said that, and fortunately for us, cars disappear much more quickly than stories.

Marcelino stumbled across the old car when he came down from the mine looking for somewhere to drink; this little trickle of water near the mine, whose huge hulk lay there like the skeleton of some prehistoric animal, was the very same stream that had been diverted so that mining could begin.

The car didn't have a windscreen or windows, or an engine, or any wheels of course, but it was much better than the cave. He padded out the interior with dry grass and covered the outside with hazel branches, camouflaging it so well that if anyone thought to look for him around there, they wouldn't find him even if they were standing right in front of him. It was warm and dry inside. There was plenty of water nearby, and little trout that he would catch with his hands and roast skewered on a stick. Above his head, the trees formed a canopy so dense that the smoke chose to wend its way out through the woods rather than rise up to the sky, and the fire couldn't be seen from far away at night. No. If they found him it wouldn't be because he'd given away his whereabouts, or because someone had followed the old road the car had driven along on its journey to this graveyard of forgetful elephants.

We rather like Lino's hiding place. It's easy to imagine that beneath those trees, in that forest, lie buried cities, motorways, entire civilizations, and that Lino is the sole survivor. Time has ceased to exist or has been reborn.

* * *

We also know you, who you were. And how you used to like to come back to the village now and again to see those who'd stayed behind. They'd be fat, old, and uncouth, with several kids in tow who never gave them a second's peace. It was your victory, your confirmation that you'd done the right thing by leaving as soon as you could and for good, for the city, on the pretext that you were off to study something or other. It was proof that you'd gotten ahead. You, the humble offspring of farmers and country bumpkins, had made it. You were writing for online magazines, you were going to trendy bars, you had umpteen boyfriends and girlfriends and one-night stands. You were creative, free, ironic, and above all modern. You were superior beings. Even if you couldn't make ends meet because nobody paid you for your works of genius. Even if you were constantly depressed and none of your relationships lasted more than a few months and you felt dreadfully lonely in your poky rooms in shared apartments or in your minuscule studios with views onto an ugly air shaft and a disappointing future. At the start of this journey, you were convinced they were the savages and you were the glorious colonizers civilizing the world. But over time, once the shine had worn off, you slowly came to the sad realization that in fact the savages were you, and that you'd sold off the land of your forebears in return for a couple of mirrors, some cheap plastic stuff, and a few electronic devices.

Still, you walked around the village in your fancy modern clothes so that everyone could admire you, like the *indianos*, emigrants from these parts who, over a century ago, set sail for the Americas, to return years later with their newfound riches. Whenever people asked what you did, you hesitated as if their language didn't have a word for your profession, and then said something in English, or something technical or made-up, which would leave them open-mouthed.

It must be said that you also went back to see your families. Your poor mothers, who used to miss you so much they'd call weekly to tell you that some old woman who you'd forgotten existed had died, try to pin you down on your vague plans, and make you promise to visit soon, which you'd always put off till Christmas, Easter, or summer, because, goddammit Mom, I've got tons of work to do.

You were never going to move back but visiting felt great. Yes. On the one hand you were admired, defined, and strong by comparison; on the other, protected and spoiled. But you never stayed more than a week before flying off again toward progress. Except this time, when you decided to come back because for once the crowd—the youngsters who'd arrived in your village en masse—was young and hip, and after a concerted effort on your part you were accepted into the fold. This time you flaunted your native status. This time at least your mothers were happy, because you were home for a long stay.

* * *

This is where we are: today there was no sound or light or darkness, as a thick fog had blotted out the world, and all that remained were Marcelino and the two square yards around him.

He listened in silence to the crackling wood in the fire he'd lit not so much for warmth as to prevent the fog from stealing all the colors. There was no sun in the sky, and he had no idea what time it was. He couldn't do anything, not even go away and come back when everything returned, but he felt calm, because if the world didn't exist, his brother didn't either.

And since time didn't exist, we don't know how long he was asleep.

* * *

He was woken by a dog barking. The cotton wool all around him was whiter now, and the fog was drawing back, satiated with absence. He heard the barking again, and this time he recognized it. More barking. It seemed close.

* * *

He found it about three hundred yards away, by the road. The dog squirmed, growled, and pulled hard on the chain when it saw him. Marcelino looked around, but there was no one there except the frightened animal tied to a tree, and beside it a bowl of food.

The fog had left him half deaf, like when someone you love dies, so the sound he could hear was extremely faint, like electricity cables in the wind or a branch about to break. He crept closer and saw a strange metal box attached to a tree.

And finally you, we, all of us saw him. All dirty, his clothes, skin, and hair still covered in red smudges. He had grass tangled in his beard and hair. His shining black eyes betrayed fear and curiosity as he peered out from our screens and televisions, from the internet, social media, from the headline summary on the news, from the front pages, and we understood, a little guiltily, that it was all real, and yes, Marcelino was afraid and had absolutely no idea what was happening.

Then he stepped back, untied his dog, and exited screen left.

* * *

Along came fire and burned the stick that killed the dog that ate the cat that ate the mouse that ate the cheese that was all the old woman and the old man had to eat.

* * *

But the truth is that the forest believed Marcelino had been born there, like the rotten fence, the holes in the oaks' trunks, the bear skeleton, the dried fox pelt, the bone fragments in the medieval pit where plague victims had been dumped, the heart-like nests in the chests of the trees, or the ruins of the great mill—now nothing but a hollow in the ground beside the waterfall, with a few moss-covered stones in a circle around it—which in times gone by would have been the pride of these villages. And so he made no sound as he moved through the brambles and the bushes; he didn't crunch loudly through the dead leaves, he didn't frighten the animals, the trees didn't tremble as he passed, and the crows didn't fly off screeching from the uppermost branches. He'd become part of the forest, like young couples who have just made love, like poets, like fools and children, like saints. But as soon as someone other than him set foot here, it would be like a stone falling into a still lake: the ripples at the water's edge would give them away. And if it was also nighttime, and they were carrying lamps, they'd have no chance of taking him by surprise.

They were turning the car over, taking what was inside, picking up the food remains, staring into the glowing embers of the fire, as if they couldn't believe it. Marcelino was watching them from his hiding place among the enormous roots of a huge fallen chestnut tree on the banks of the stream, about twenty yards away. They were no longer whispering or rushing along like a mad gust of wind dragging everything with it and snapping masses of dry twigs. Now they were talking loudly, and they'd turned on a big searchlight.

Marcelino picked up his bag and stepped into the stream, ready to leave. The cold, dark water came up to his knees. But then his dog saw a wild boar and barked.

The searchlight spun round toward him. Several people were shouting. He started running. They ordered him to stop and waded in after him. He took out his pistol and without turning round pressed the trigger twice. The shots rang out like explosions and the bullets soared straight up into the sky without even grazing a branch. Six further shots sounded, hitting the trunk of a beech tree with beautiful red leaves, a large white rock, the clay riverbed, and lastly his dog, which died instantly.

Marcelino ran. He ran downhill, following the course of the stream. He tripped and fell. He got up, scratching his face on some branches. He ran until the stream flowed into a river, and he kept on running through the river. He ran for hours; in his mind the sounds of his own splashing feet became confused with those of his pursuers. He even thought he could still hear gunshots, getting closer and closer.

When he finally stopped running, dawn was breaking. He lay down exhausted and shivering on the bank. From the depths of sleep, he opened his eyes for a second and saw, between the branches, an enormous bird flapping its wings in the sky. It looked like a dragon.

* * *

There were still old folk in San Antolín who would tell the time by the sun. History doesn't come to villages, or, if it does, only briefly, like a visitor who has to leave first thing in the morning. There can be no such thing as history when all the chapters belong to an ancient and holy book, full of endlessly repeating plots and characters. History, your history, belongs in cities, like the sewers.

Naturally, there were sad stories from the last war, but people would tell them as if they'd happened the week before and everyone knew the characters, as if the past were simply a neighboring hamlet and the world and everything you needed to know of it fitted neatly between the slopes of the valley. Which, come to think of it, is true.

* * *

Like the tale of Juan el del Rusco, who was too clever for his own good.

Juan lived on the outskirts of the village, in the first house if you're coming from León.

At the beginning of the war, the village, which had no strategic importance whatsoever, played host to a continuous stream of small units of soldiers on their way to one front or another. Small groups would arrive from time to time and shoot the odd dog to shake people up a bit. They would go into one of the farmsteads, consume everything like a fever, and spend the night there before setting off again for Villar, Oviedo, or Lugo. Most of them were young lads from places just like San Antolín who were tired of marching toward their deaths—they wanted to forget, to eat, to drink, and maybe share a few jokes by the fireside—and if they hadn't requisitioned the chickens, the cheeses, and any other food they could lay their hands on, they wouldn't have been much of a bother.

Juan el del Rusco was too clever by half, though. He realized that whenever the Republicans left, the Nationalists would arrive, and vice versa, and so as soon as any troops appeared on the road he would come out of the house shouting "Viva la República!" or "Viva Franco!" to get on the right side of them, so that they wouldn't give him any trouble or steal his chickens.

But the story goes that one day they turned up as it was getting dark, when he'd just gotten home from the bar a little worse for wear. He could hear their footsteps on the gravel path, but he couldn't see them properly. All the same, he shouted "Viva Franco!" at which there was a stunned silence, as he'd put his foot in it and this group wasn't in fact Nationalists at all. When he realized his mistake, he started shouting that he had no interest in politics, and that he was a simpleton and didn't know what he was saying, to which a sergeant retorted that if he knew nothing about politics why was he expressing an opinion, and shot him on the spot.

This happened more than seventy years ago, but everyone in the village knows the story and they all tell it. And they laugh, because it's funny, obviously.

* * *

Or like the tale of Conchita la Marquesona, who, despite her nickname, had very little of the marchioness about her aside from her airs and graces. She was, however, abundantly mad.

Young woman that she was, while everyone else shut themselves away in their houses, she went out on her own to greet the Nationalist troops when they arrived in the parish, and applauded, shouting, "At long last God and Country have returned, at long last the Holy Apostolic Roman Church has returned!" But the Moroccan soldiers who made up most of the army knew precious little about the Holy Apostolic Roman Church. The only thanks she got was to be raped for hours; they decided to partake of her body rather than of her insane rallying cries.

When this story is told in these parts everyone laughs because, again, it's meant to be funny, and they add that Conchita, who died of old age not long ago, remained a religious fanatic and fervent Franco supporter throughout her life. Mind you, from that point on, she hated Arabs.

* * *

Stories such as these were what used to constitute History, not Mussolini or Hitler, who weren't from the village. And these stories would intermingle with others from the same period. A period that spanned thousands of years yet would fit neatly between one sip of wine and the next, into the blink of an eye, into a memory that flashes through your mind, into a snippet of gossip.

That's all for today. Our gaze is more inward than outward. Let's say goodbye to our friends, close the door and get into bed, turn off the light: the fire is going out. More stories tomorrow.

* * *

They used to say that if you slept outside under a full moon you'd grow hair all over your body, and big fangs, and you'd prowl around cemeteries and desecrate tombs in search of flesh. You were saying that perhaps Marcelino was killed while trying to escape. They used to say that if the moonlight shone on you while you were dreaming, it would possess you and lead you into a forest from which you'd never escape. You were saying that surely he must have been hit by a bullet, surely he'd eventually have died from blood loss. That the moon would shine a light on the parts of our soul that were best kept hidden in the dark. That he must have died in some hollow by the river or even that his body was floating, lifeless like a log, tangled up in the weeds near the bank. That if you were a woman, you'd give birth to sharp-fanged wolf-children who would never be satisfied by your milk because they'd need blood. And if you were an old woman you'd prowl around your neighbors' houses on a full moon and sneak in through a window and steal their children, later slaughtering them in a clearing in the forest. And after smearing your naked body with their fresh blood, you'd devour them. You were saying that if he managed to keep going for a couple of miles before collapsing, perhaps he reached the point where the stream joins the Neva and his body was swept out to sea. At least at this time of year the river wouldn't be too high, and it would be easier to find him. Not to mention the fig trees, which old folk and children should steer clear of at any time, but on a full moon you'd have to flee as if the trees were Satan himself, because their thick white sap fed on the moonlight. It's no coincidence that Judas chose this tree to hang himself.

Sap of a fig tree, semen from hanged men in the earth, white moonlight, a mother's milk that's poison to us.

* * *

But *his* mother would never say any of this. His mother liked to gaze at the full moon, and she would assure him that it was turning our souls a soft caramel color while it smiled on us. The Moon was the daughter of the Oak and the Sun and was in love with the River. And Marcelino's father was the black shadowless night. The swarm of stupid, angry flies.

* * *

The trees were leaning inquisitively over the still pool in the river, watching him sleep. He awoke as if he were coming back to life. An icy chill ran through him. Then a hunger pang. He reached into his bag and found that the water had spoiled nearly all the food. He took bites from the chorizo and ate some blackberries from the riverbank. He undressed, spread his clothes out to dry in the sun in a clearing and lay down. His skin was gleaming white, like a pebble from a well.

He wasn't in the New World or the old one; he'd transcended all frontiers. He looked in vain for the rocky mass of the Cordillera Central. He looked to see where the moss was growing, so he could work out which way was south. He gazed in silence at the dense clouds sailing across the sky, the breeze moving through the grassland.

Cutting across the meadow was a strip of slightly shorter grass that didn't reflect the sunlight as much. He dug down a little and found traces of fine white gravel. It was an abandoned footpath, hidden by time. Naturally, he followed it. A rotten gate led him into some woods, where he came across a rusty iron bench beside a great oak tree and saw a little iron bandstand so corroded that it looked as if it were made from those tiny wires placed around champagne corks. He left the woods and arrived at a grassy hill.

* * *

A lush beard of ivy had grown over almost the entire façade; only the big windows, the balconies, and the front door were left uncovered. It looked like a face watching his approach with a stern expression. The roof had yawning holes in it.

The corridor walls were decorated with a green frieze, now almost indistinguishable from the mildew tarnishing the once brilliant white paint. The wooden floor creaked beneath his weight like the hull of an ancient ship in a storm. In places the roof had started to cave in, and a tangled mess of rods and slats protruded like a scarecrow's guts. There were dismantled iron beds, mattresses, bedside tables, wardrobes, enameled chamber pots, all piled up to one side in the large bedrooms, as if someone had tried to make space or had been preparing for a move that never happened. In a few rooms, with white-tiled walls and marble everywhere, stood huge bathtubs filled with dead leaves, fossilized insects, and earth. The light from the windows in these rooms was endlessly reflected like falling snow, like a childhood memory. You could feel the pain.

And around all sides of the building, a large and long-neglected garden. Shrubs whose roots had burst out, shattering their pots; stone steps covered by grass; marble tables buried in undergrowth; withered fruit trees and overgrown fruit trees; all of it caged in by thorny brambles as thick as a child's wrist, as if they were there to ensure that no one woke the princess from her enchanted sleep; and an enormous acacia that looked as if it might come crashing down and bring everything to its inevitable conclusion.

* * *

He found a pile of white sheets in a wardrobe and laid them over a mattress. He lay down and listened. The wind blowing through this empty skull, this boat washed up on a strange shore; a faint echo of dripping water; tattered curtains flapping in the breeze; the leaves on the trees like waves breaking on an empty beach. The sheets smelled of dampness, of earth, of shrouds, of crypts, of rotting wood.

He slept until dusk, when the cold woke him. He picked up some pieces of old parquet flooring and some rotten wool and laid a fire in one of the white rooms. The dancing flames were reflected in the tiles. The smoke rose to the top of the high ceilings and escaped through the hallways full of invisible currents. The whole building gave a little shudder, like a mummy whose heart has sprung to life, like a bird after a storm when the sun comes out.

The sky through the windows was gray and dull like old cement.

When night fell, the smells awoke and came in to keep him company along with the sound of the nearby river, the crickets and the toads reciting their spells. Everything around him had forgotten humankind's existence and did not fear him.

A tawny owl hooted in a nearby tree at the same time as thousands of muezzins in their minarets were calling the faithful to prayer in thousands of Arab villages and cities.

* * *

It was a miracle too when light came to Villar. In the town square they erected great iron streetlamps emblazoned with the municipality's shield.

When the day arrived, people came flooding down from

all the villages, some on horseback, some in carts, most of them on foot with wicker baskets full of food on their heads, and hanging from their arms too. It was a proper *romería* festival. The well-to-do families looked down on the mass of human bodies from their balconies. Folding chairs were set out by the town hall for the special guests and the old folk. Little children were playing and running and screeching in great flocks, like their friends the swallows once did in the summer sky. Some men were singing. Some were smoking, and the smoke was floating up like incense in the clear air. Some were fiddling with their mustaches and beards. Some were nervously turning their berets in their hands like steering wheels. The laughter, like the cider, had started going to people's heads when the first stars started blinking in the reddening sky. Babies were asleep in their mothers' arms. As night fell and jackets were being draped over shoulders, the hubbub gradually lowered by two octaves, as if everyone were praying. Then a door opened on the town hall balcony, which had a Spanish flag draped over its balustrade, and the mayor stepped out to cheers from some, jeers from others, and mocking laughter from most, like the laughter of children when they see a man wearing blackface to play Balthazar in the Three Kings procession. The mayor said a few words, hoping to engrave his name on the great tombstone of history, but nobody was listening and in the end he simply cried: "To progress!"

And then the streetlamps came on, their light as yellow and bright as a thousand candles. Everyone stood open-mouthed and wide-eyed, as if an angel had appeared. Then they let out an "*Oooh*." And lastly, people began to clap, which soon turned into a huge round of applause for the future.

Ramón el del Molín was silent. His small eyes, buried in his ninety-year-old face, were shining. He was sitting down, his hands tightly clasped around the top of his walking stick. But Amor, Carroceda's little one, spotted a tear rolling down his furrowed cheek and pointed it out to her mother, who cheerfully asked him whether he was sad or had something in his eye. Ramón rapped the ground once with his stick as though he wanted to hammer it in.

"I've seen the day by night: now I can die in peace," he said, his voice barely a whisper.

* * *

If truth be told, Quique is fifty years old, but depending on the day he'll tell you that he's three or a hundred. Nobody knows for sure if he's being serious or if it's a game he never tires of playing.

Some people in the village think he's a trickster and not the slightest bit mad.

You still see him around San Antolín occasionally, but for a while now he's been living in Gijón, where he has an apartment he pays for with his disability benefit and where he can make a lot more money begging in the streets. You'll often find him sitting on a bench, surrounded by an enraptured crowd. Usually they're female, for the most part insecure teenagers, but even though he could, he never sleeps with any of them.

One time, a lad he'd asked for money in the street retorted angrily that he was broke and unemployed. At this Quique took out a bundle of notes and insisted the lad take it to help him pass his final school exams. The boy was the sole witness to this, but everyone knows about it.

Before Marcelino killed his brother, Quique was without doubt the most famous person in the village. He'd even made the international news. This is his story:

Twenty-five years ago, when he was still a prophet-in-training, he had a series of premonitions that tormented him night after night, and so he disappeared from the village. For a long while nothing was heard of him, to the point where everyone assumed he'd died. But one morning he reappeared in a most unexpected place: on the front pages of the newspapers.

The photo showed Quique lying on the floor, held down by two bodyguards. Two other men and a police officer in a helmet, the kind the British wear, had their weapons trained on him. Quique's cheek was pressed flat against the tarmac and his neck was tensed. He had a hand on his head and a knee pinning his back, and his mouth was open in a cry of surrender and pain. The news report explained that Quique had jumped through security and thrown himself on the Princess of Wales, who was on an official visit to Plymouth.

According to Quique, his intention hadn't been to kill her or indeed to do her any harm whatsoever. In fact, he was trying to save her, as God had told him in his dreams that this beautiful British woman was going to be assassinated, and that he'd been chosen to warn her.

By midday all the newspapers in the municipality had sold out. And though the news had everyone in fits of laughter, deep down they were all very proud of their famous lunatic and they all turned up to welcome him back when he was repatriated.

Some people in the village think he's a trickster and not the slightest bit mad.

When the television stations called to ask him to talk about his crazy adventure, not only did he refuse to do so for free like a loser, but he became quite hard-nosed and sold his story to the highest bidder. When they decided to build a sports center, people suggested that the new street be named after him.

The thing is, nobody knows whether he's a trickster or a lunatic. What they do know is that he's the only one who can put his hand through the bars of the Villa Conchita without getting his arm bitten off by the three Doberman guard dogs. At first people tried to warn him not to do it. But he always replied that they wouldn't bite him because they knew who he was. And he was right: anyone else and they'd have killed him, but he could pet them like they were puppies.

You'd often see him around the village in those days. Some of the boys, who were looking for something they couldn't quite articulate, found what they needed in him— the clown, the wandering scholar, the faun, the village shaman. And though Quique didn't even know Marcelino, all the journalists asked his opinion, which he was only too happy to provide.

By the way, the Princess of Wales, Lady Di, died in a suspicious car accident a few years after Quique attempted to warn her.

* * *

"Out of the embraces of the Moon and the River a pale little girl was born who was loved by the animals and the plants. The little girl gave everything a name. Different names from the ones we know now, as there were no letters and each word was itself part of what it named. They were sounds, gestures, and silence. They were leaf, treetop, and tree. They were both part and whole, and everything was connected, so that if you called something, that something would lead to you to call the next thing. And words would beget words, and would give thanks for the miracle of existence to the ones who'd come before. So a flower was an open hand; and an open hand a flower in the sun and the valley basin. So night was a closed flower; and a closed flower a clenched fist and a mountain. So death was life and life death, hand and fist, open and closed, male and female, semen and ice, spring and winter. And big or small wasn't important. And near or far didn't exist. And as for above and below, good or bad, how absurd! And you could live your whole life using only one word.

"But the girl grew up and was so beautiful that *he* wanted to possess her.

"He butted a wall with his great horns, and the girl roared like an avalanche.

"He raised a great cloud of dust with his hind hooves, and the girl blew like the wind and quaked.

"He brought down a tree with his horns, and the girl laughed and thundered and put earth in her mouth.

"He showed his great penis, and the girl said *sun, spring, life, seed, moss, trunk, worm, death*.

"Eventually, after trying everything, he sat down on a rock and wept. The girl watched him and didn't understand. She moved closer to him and touched a tear. She asked:

"*River?*

"But river it wasn't.

"*Water?*

"But water it wasn't. She brought the tear to her tongue and said:

"*Sea?*

"But sea it wasn't. She looked at his face and neither was it death, nor winter, nor anything she'd ever seen.

"*What is it?* she asked, fascinated.

"*Sadness*, he answered.

"*Sadness?* she repeated, not understanding.

"*Sadness because of Love.*

"*Love?* she asked.

"And he explained it to her.

"He explained the past, on hearing which she began to miss what never was. He explained the future, at which she began to desire what would never be. And lastly, he explained the present, which made her feel trapped in a tiny space, in a nutshell sailing on a torrent. He showed her pain. He taught her of good and evil. He made her be afraid and, because of her fear, forget the true names of things.

"Then she loved him too."

* * *

And we know what we're talking about, because we know all about miracles. We've been keeping a watchful eye for thousands of years and we've witnessed them all. Because if a miracle occurs and we're not there to see it, it isn't a miracle. Light exists only because there are eyes to see what it illuminates. There can be no brilliance if no one is blinded by it.

We know that a star shone millions of years ago so that tonight a boy can point it out to a girl he loves and explain to her that, together with other stars, it makes up the constellation of Orion. Millions of years across space and an incalculable amount of energy never to be repeated, for her to smile and let him place an arm around her shoulders. We know that hundreds of thousands of millions of species of trees have begun to exist, have covered the earth and have disappeared, giving way to other forms of life in an infinitely slow and patient evolution, to create the perfect design for the sycamore seeds that, right now, are being carried by the wind, spinning around and around like tiny propellers, and that a small child is chasing, laughing as they catch one in their hand.

We know that a bird that became extinct hundreds of millions of years ago survived dinosaurs, predators, a meteorite crashing to earth and decades of pitch darkness so that hundreds of millions of years later, practically yesterday, an upright walking ape could inherit that same songbird's vocal organs, so that one unremarkable morning that first ape could contract its own vocal cords to produce a grunt or a shriek, and then repeat the same sound twice over to mean a thing, and by doing so name an object for the first time. And by naming it they could become separate from it, and distance themselves from it forever, which meant that they could take control of it. A first ape who invented a first word and so allowed, another few million years later, an old man of no particular significance to bid farewell to his loved ones before plunging into the silence broken by that first word, that miraculous word from which we all came. We know that before that, way before, there was first nothing, then babbling, then slime, fish, amphibian, lizard and bird, ape, human, so many humans surviving so many infinitesimal probabilities so that Marcelino would be born and become a child and grow up and kill his brother and love and be loved—and that way before that, someone would experience love for the very first time so that all of us could know what love is—and it would mean as much as any of these stars. We know, as we've said before, that all this, absolutely all of it, is nothing short of a miracle.

And we also know that we talk in the same way that a rock brings a landslide down with it when we drop it over a cliff. We talk so much because if we were to keep quiet we'd have to learn everything all over again. We know we talk incessantly in the hope of finding, every hundred, every thousand years, one sentence that is true, one good, simple sentence. Another miracle. We're always on the lookout.

We have time, we have all time.

We know that rosebushes move like snakes and that lakes evaporate like the morning dew, that forests are the foam of time.

We also know that each person is a simple little song that, though easily forgotten, has a beautiful refrain.

* * *

His mother went away, but she left him light. His father sleeps in the depths of the earth among jagged rocks and swarms of angry flies and comes out at night to torment him.

Marcelino.

Give me your hand.

And Marcelino gave her his hand. She was the only person who ever stroked his calloused, dirty hand.

His brother and a few neighbors from the village were drinking downstairs and he could hear their laughter. Marcelino doesn't like laughter. When people laugh, it makes him think they're hurt, or that they're about to attack him.

Marcelino.

Open the window, go on.

And Marcelino raised the blind and opened it. A soft pure light lapped at the small room where his mother had lain in bed for a few days. The incoming breeze gently caught the white cotton curtains, which in turn caressed the handful of old books, their leather spines worn smooth by the hands of his mother, upon whom they now gaze, lost in thought, from their little bookshelf. Manure, grass, and damp soil; all the aromas of the departing day came inside

116

and swept away the smell of dirty sheets, old wood, dust, and chamber pots.

Give me your hand again.

His mother closed her eyes and smiled. His mother's smile he does like. His mother never laughs, but she does smile, and, when she does, Marcelino knows nothing bad can happen.

His mother smiled as the light caressed her face, her white skin crisscrossed with fine blue veins, and the smile remained on her lips as she lay with her hand in his and her eyes closed.

The dogs barked, frightened by the dark, which crept up and filled the valleys drop by drop like black water filling a glass. The birds sang in unison, bidding farewell to the light. The dogs continued to bark, trying to scare away the shadows, afraid the day wouldn't return. The church bells intoned that once again everything had been forgiven, and somewhere nearby a cuckoo concurred. The great din of life outside, and such profound silence inside. Even his brother and the neighbors fell silent. Just Marcelino's raspy, calm breathing as he gazed at his mother's smiling face.

Something moved. Something fell to the floor. A cow in labor bellowed in the distance like a Viking horn at the end of the battle. The scraping of chairs. Footsteps on the creaking stairs. The door opening.

She's dead, whispered the priest, crossing himself as if he'd been caught red-handed, and to Marcelino it sounded like a crow cawing.

His mother left with the light, smiling, and she comes back with it to smile at him. When night falls, she bids him farewell.

* * *

Yes: nowadays we're all beautiful. Our immaculate skin, our delicate hands, our wise eyes brimming with life and happiness. But until recently beauty was the preserve of the aristocracy, at least of the aristocrats who weren't inbred or hadn't simply been painted by an accomplished court artist with a special talent for flattery; or possibly of the occasional country girl in her prime before the icy temperatures, the heat, and six children left her aged and blemished, like a ripened blue cheese; and, most of all, beauty was the preserve of virgins, angels, and saints. Their likenesses would induce in the poor, the ugly, and the deformed a state of ecstasy—a mixture of devotion, admiration, and desire.

For this reason we're almost tempted to say that in San Antolín a shabby porn photo was passed from house to house. But what was actually passed around was a miniature chapel with a little virgin inside, and it was assigned to each family for a few days each year.

When it was closed it looked like a wooden box with a handle, the case of a humble shoeshine boy. But once it was opened, a series of unfolding parts fitted together to form an altar with a decorative frontispiece and carved arches, where the little statue of a beautiful virgin stood behind a glass pane, her hand raised in a gesture of benediction, surrounded by dried flowers: the Virgin Mary.

As if it were a children's book, the youngest in the house were usually the ones permitted to open the box. Sadly, they weren't allowed to close it again so that they could reopen it, then close it again and open it once more, which is what they'd like to have done. It wasn't a toy, and next time it was folded away it would be to fulfill the devotional needs of other villagers.

At the base, on this side of the glass and at the Virgin's feet, was a metal coin slot. There was no obligation to donate, as it had been paid for generations ago by all the neighbors jointly, but every time it arrived at a new house, even before opening it they would shake it gently, almost unconsciously, to see if they could hear a lot of coins in the mystical money box. This was almost always the case, to everyone's annoyance, and meant they'd have to keep up with the neighbors by adding to its weight, which they always did, with a quip from the man of the house—"This thing earns more than me," "We could buy our own with the amount we put in," "The priest won't be short of the blood of Christ this year," etc.—before Grandma gasped in horror, crossed herself and later giggled mischievously.

In the beginning, it must have been all polished and glossy, but it soon started to look a little shabby, a little dusty, as though that were its natural state. And then there was the smoke from cigarettes and hearths and the soot; the passage of time and the passing from hand to hand; the villagers shaking it to weigh up the extent of their neighbors' generosity; the variations in temperature, sorrows and pleas, depressions and confessions. All these things soon took their toll on the lovely lady, who, to tell the truth, reminded the latest generation of little girls of Barbie in her caravan. The box was showing signs of woodworm and there were grease marks on its sides, the dried flowers were as thin and brittle as a shed snakeskin, plus their tips were broken off, and worst of all: one of the statue's delicate little hands had been chipped away, leaving only a stump, almost as if it had bestowed too many blessings.

For one hundred and fifty-seven years it revolved around the entire valley non-stop like an unclaimed suitcase. The first people to pray to her passed away, but the Virgin lived on. Those who prayed to her later on also left us, and it was their children's turn to receive her into their homes. Each family became several families, each branch produced more branches and some died out, and she was admired by all the children; she listened to hundreds of thousands of after-dinner conversations, countless chiming living-room clocks and a chorus of cockerels announcing new dawns; she witnessed the hopes and dreams of people who have long since stopped dreaming, the true queen of all things small. Until, fifteen years ago, she came up against a closed door because the old lady who'd been looking after her had died the previous winter, and while nobody had anything against the Virgin, nobody thought to send her to the next home either. They simply let her fall into oblivion, like a trusty old farm tool that nobody throws out but that, well, nobody uses any more.

So what happened was that, not long ago, Ángeles, daughter of Ana la de Ca Pando, who'd returned to the Pando household from Madrid for the holidays right at the point all the fuss was kicking off, was thinking about all those excited kids gathering in the village streets and needing something to believe in, when, all at once, she remembered the Virgin and how much she'd liked her as a child. Ángeles was lying in her bed, about to drop off, in that cold and saggy childhood bed that seemed to want to hug her, like all beds back home. She realized that she'd never learned what had happened to the Virgin, and that she'd not seen anything like her since, except possibly the fold-out boxes full of weapons used by vampire hunters in Hollywood B movies to dispatch the bad guys, and she laughed at the thought. It was then that, as if she had the wooden box right there with her in the dark, its smell came back to her clear as anything. The smell of old wood, dusty flowers, cabbage stew, floor wax, bleach, confessional, and warm hearth. A humble, tender, peaceful, safe smell. The smell of newborn kittens in a cardboard box at the back of a wardrobe. The smell of kind, old hands stroking a grand-daughter's cheek. The smell of saintliness. That was when she broke down and wept like she hadn't wept in years.

The next morning, she went to the church to ask about the Virgin. The priest, a young man responsible for no fewer than seven parishes since the death of Father Alfonso, his predecessor—parishioners and religious calling were in equally short supply—claimed he'd never seen her, but he was intrigued by the young woman's beautiful description and together they ended up searching for her in the storage room, hunting through broken plaster saints, trunks full of moldy clothes, moth-eaten missals, countless Nativity figurines, baptism books, half-burned candles, bent-double candles, candle stumps, braziers and incense burners made of copper and tin, woodworm-ridden pews and prayer kneelers, rickety chairs, rubbish, rotting matter, junk, and even a little white coffin that looked like a box of sweets. They didn't find her, of course.

* * *

Nobody knows what they were.

They appeared one especially hot summer. The summer of '85, if we remember rightly.

Sara la del Maestro said she saw one crawling on the kitchen tiles, so she picked it up with a piece of paper and threw it out of the window without giving it a second thought. That same night, so they said, the same thing happened in several houses. But by the following morning there were already so many you couldn't help but notice them. In the beginning a lot of people were afraid it was a plague that would devour their crops, but they soon discovered that if they were feeding on anything, it was nothing anyone knew about. They were just crawling, seemingly without destination or purpose, as if they were lost.

A few days later the sheer quantity of them was quite alarming. The road and the walls were mottled with them, although admittedly, except in a few instances, they weren't venturing inside the houses, nor did they appear keen on fields or nature. Preferring to crawl and multiply in open spaces, they seemed oblivious to our existence. They had no need of us, if they even needed anything at all, except for us to build them tarmac and concrete roads.

They were worms, or larvae, or caterpillars, fat and white, the size of your little finger. Not even the oldest person in the village had ever seen anything like it.

A week later there were so many you couldn't walk without squashing one at every step. The road was a viscous mass of worms crushed by car tires. You couldn't make out any internal organs; they would simply burst like a skin full of milk.

The mayor even called SEPRONA, the Nature Protection Service.

"But are they doing any harm? Are they eating the pasture? The vegetable plots?" asked a woman in the office.

"No, they don't seem to be, but there are a lot of them."

"Well, in that case they'll soon be gone. If their behavior changes, don't hesitate to let us know, thank you," said the woman and hung up, leaving the mayor completely bewildered. All of which led to much speculation, and in the bar everyone was talking about it.

Isabel la de Ramona said she'd seen one of those planes they use for putting out fires spraying "something very strange" on a nearby hillside, but nobody believed her because, aside from her not having mentioned it before, as if she'd literally only just remembered, she'd also claimed on other occasions to have seen the Virgin Mary, the *Santa Compaña* ghosts of local legend, and even Martians landing in the churchyard. Not to mention that whenever something went missing in her house, or she lost the most trifling thing, she would say enigmatically that someone was "playing games" with her.

Paco el del Estudiante declared that it was a new plague, a bug that had appeared from nowhere because of pollution and the incredibly hot weather, most likely because of a hole in the ozone layer above our village. He said we'd have to wait and see how it "evolved." This theory, though somewhat disconcerting, was the most widely accepted.

At the start we worried that the stench of so many rotting corpses would make the air unbreathable, but the days went by and the thousands of squashed carcasses mounted up and they didn't seem to give off any odor at all. Their skins, whitish membranes, would simply shrivel up and disintegrate before being swept away like paper on the wind, while the liquid would shimmer in the sun like a snail trail. Soon afterward it too would disappear, with not even a hint of the smell of rotting flesh.

Ramoncín el de Pacho, who was a cocky little know-it-all, threw himself into scientific research, which basically meant subjecting the worms to every kind of torture imaginable. And yet, it must be said, the results were quite remarkable.

He took a worm and impaled it on a hook to try fishing with it, but he observed that none of the trout were swimming up to it. If anything, the fish seemed to deliberately steer clear. He also noticed that the birds didn't eat them.

He took another and put it in the mouth of his dog, who spat it out and ran away whimpering. Next, he ground some up with a pestle and mortar and threw them to the chickens. They weren't keen either.

He sealed a worm in a vacuum, in one of the glass jars people use to store chorizos in oil, and it turned out they didn't need air to breathe.

He tried giving them all sorts of things to eat, and they didn't eat anything.

He put two in a box to see if they would reproduce. He didn't spot any sign of physical activity, but every morning they'd doubled in number.

This was all very surprising, and the whole village was talking about it. Truthfully, they were a bit scared when Ramoncín, so he claimed, threw some in the fire and they didn't burn, although everyone said that this last part was a lie, and that he'd gotten carried away because he was enjoying all the attention. In any case, it was clear that the worms were of no use for anything, but they weren't asking for anything either, except space, and so, apart from the revulsion they instilled, apart from inquisitive children and clumsy humans, their species had no predators or enemies. The kids in the village named them "nitwit worms," to show they weren't scared of them.

"Are those worms still there?" the woman from SEPRONA asked the mayor on the phone some time later.

"Yes, they're still here. And there are more and more of them," he answered.

"Still not doing any harm?"

"No, except they're revolting, but no, they're not doing any harm and they're not going into houses."

"Do you know any more about them?"

"Yes. Nothing eats them, not birds, not fish. They seem to have nothing inside except liquid. They don't rot. They don't eat anything. They multiply without anyone understanding how. And, the most unbelievable thing of all, if you throw them in the fire they don't burn!" said the mayor, sure that this would impress her.

"Uh-huh, I see. Well, if anything changes, sir, please don't hesitate to call." And with that she put the phone down.

Nevertheless, one day two men turned up in a van. They were wearing medical gowns and could be seen walking around the village. They put some nitwits in a jar. Some kids asked them if they were government investigators, but they simply smiled, eventually leaving in much the same way they'd arrived, just like that, never to return.

In fact, except for the mayor, who couldn't cope with any more village goings-on beyond his control, and except for the odd religious nut who feared it was a punishment from God—a completely absurd punishment, obviously—nobody was too worried, and before long everyone had gotten used to the road being white, as though it had been snowing in the middle of August.

Village folk don't tend to like it when something new comes along, but once it's happened, it doesn't take long for them to accept it and even feel grateful for a bit of a change.

It wasn't until three weeks later that the fear set in.

* * *

It wasn't until three weeks later that the fear set in.

Sancho el del Pontigo died, of old age, and everyone went to the funeral because people were so fond of him. Several young lads carried his coffin on their shoulders from the church to the cemetery, roughly half a mile. Because they were taking tiny steps and the procession following them was forced to go at the same pace, a horrendous number of worms was massacred and the squelching underfoot was rather unpleasant. Lina de Olegario, who was very religious, kept making the sign of the cross and saying it was the work of the Devil. And they all sniggered quietly, because it wasn't the sort of thing you laughed about out loud.

But as they passed through the cemetery gates they too got a fright. Not because there were more worms there; it was an open space, after all, plus the ground in the cemetery was concrete and desolate—perfect conditions for the worms to proliferate further, if that were even possible—and the villagers weren't the kind to cry over spilled milk. No, the reason they were so frightened was quite the opposite: there wasn't a single worm to be seen. They were amassing in the road by the entrance and alongside the walls, but not going in. The cemetery was plague-free. As if there were a glass door or some force repelling them. As if something were driving them away.

They buried Sancho with more haste than felt right. Even Alfonso, the priest, was nervous and gabbling through the prayers, trying to get them over with as quickly as possible. Inside the cemetery, with all the nitwits swarming at the entrance, there was a sense of foreboding. They felt that even though the absence of worms was natural, it was unnatural that the unnatural couldn't achieve its objectives. So as soon as the coffin was in the burial niche, everyone ran out, delighted to be trampling worms again.

Father Alfonso began to take it seriously after that. Until then it had been something that science, not he, should explain, but now it was inexplicable whichever way you looked at it, and Christian sacred spaces had been brought into the mix. The correlation was undeniable. It was as if a girl you've never really noticed suddenly says she could never have a crush on you because you're ugly. You'll definitely notice her after that. And the worms had called God's cemetery ugly. So the priest listened to the righteous and announced that over the following days he would recite special prayers until the creatures vanished. He even went so far as to threaten to bring the holy statues out on parade. I can only suppose this threat was directed at the nitwits!

And that was when it happened: Conchita's two-month-old son died, just like that. He'd been perfectly fine when they left him sleeping in his bed that night. When they woke up early the next morning, they realized he'd gone for a long time without crying for his milk. He passed away silently, without crying or complaining.

I don't know how people knew this, as Conchita was such a nervous wreck that she couldn't speak, and her husband was in no mood for silly nonsense, but a few hours later they were saying that the baby's lips and chubby little cheeks had been stained white, as if he'd been vomiting when he died. Nor do

I know who first suggested that it wasn't his mother's milk but the liquid from inside the worms, because apparently it didn't smell like milk and the parts of it that had dried were shimmering. But anyway, the news spread fast and fear struck the hearts of all the families with children. And everyone shuddered when Tino pointed out that, up close, the worms' heads looked like pale nipples. They looked like a goat's teats. The Devil's Milk, they said. Nipples without love. The Devil's Breasts. The Devil suckling the children while the adults were sleeping, so that he could steal away our future.

* * *

The women prayed all night by their children's cribs, to make sure none of the worms could get anywhere near them. Their husbands mounted a guard, blocking the road in front of their houses. The whole village turned out to join in the nitwit trampling. By daybreak there'd been no further deaths, but as they'd been on watch they concluded not that the theory had been a load of nonsense, but that the very fact that no new tragedy had come to pass was proof that their prayers and their vigilance had worked. And since the church and the priest had proved to be totally useless, or possibly going for a belt-and-braces approach, some of the parents, exhausted and puffy-eyed, went to see Marcelino's mother that same morning.

* * *

The whole village congregated on the school field. Nervous energy and anxiety filled the air and spread from one group to another at such a rate that if burning witches hadn't been outlawed, I reckon they might have built a pyre and burned any old woman at the stake. But in this case, the witch was one of the good ones, and they needed a solution from her, any solution, whatever it might be, to the Devil's worms.

They were all talking at once and nobody could make themselves heard. During all this she remained silent. She was wearing black, as she had done since her brute of a husband died a few years earlier. Marcelino, already a young man, was at her side, watching them in silence, as he always did, as if somehow looking inward. Finally, she held up her hands and everyone fell silent. But she didn't say anything, she simply lifted her head and sniffed the air. She pointed toward all the villagers with a serious expression on her face. Then she crouched down and picked up a handful of earth, which she crumbled between her fingers and examined carefully before throwing it on the ground. The people were watching these strange gestures respectfully. At last, she spoke:

"The men who want to live forever have been here," she said. "Yes, they've been in the village, and they've envied you all. They've envied your food, your houses, your smiles, your hours, your days, your weather, your entire life. You see, they'll never be able to have it. And they envy you so much they don't want you to have a future. I can smell it in the unhealthy air. I can see it in the sick earth. I can see it in these worms, which aren't worms but envy. These worms are an envy so intense it has become flesh. They feed on your energy, as the mistletoe feeds on the sap of its host until it has bled it dry. These men have cast the evil eye over the whole village."

There was a sharp intake of breath at this last claim, which was the only one that made any sense to them and was all they needed to know. Afterward, some of the women sighed and made the sign of the cross, the young men smiled nervously, trying to look brave, cries of "woe is me" floated up to the heavens, and eyes sought out other eyes in an attempt to capture the fear and acceptance of the other.

"And what can we do?" a few voices asked. She didn't respond.

"Yes, tell us what we can do, woman," said the mayor.

She thought it over, stroking her chin and sniffing the air again, and finally she raised her finger as before.

"I need you to bring me a barrel full of many liters of rainwater. It must be rainwater. Also firewood, and a cooking pot or a pan. And a rod of tin and a kilo of salt."

Night was closing in by the time they'd brought everything. Rainwater had seemed impossible at first because it hadn't rained for weeks, until they remembered the tank the gutters flowed into at the Chirulo house; it collected all the rain to water the vegetable plot. The tin was easy, as it was still used for all sorts of things in the countryside.

She threw three handfuls of salt into the barrel of water and made the sign of the cross. She used the wood to build a fire. She put the pot on the fire, and the tin in the pot. She stirred the tin slowly, muttering something nobody could understand. The flames lit up the silent, anxious faces of those around her. When the tin had melted and was bubbling, she took the pot off the fire and carried it over to the barrel. She made the sign of the cross over the barrel with the pot and poured out some of the contents, which on making contact with the water hissed like a giant snake, giving everyone goosebumps. This she repeated three more times, until she'd emptied all of the tin from the pot. She put her hands in the water and washed her face with it. Afterward, she turned round with a smile on her face, at which the people let out a sigh of relief.

"Yes, that's it. Now you must all wash your faces with this water. When you're done, throw the rest on the road, all over the worms, and one of you must recite, 'With time you came, with time shall you leave. I have no fear of you now, nitwit, Satan. You will not live here.' Lastly, take the remaining pieces of solid tin and bury them in front of the church, and smash the barrel into small pieces. If you do this, nothing bad will happen to you from now on and in two weeks the worms will be gone."

One by one they began washing their faces, and they all smiled contentedly afterward. They washed the babies too, and the mounting laughter mingled with the cries of the newly saved.

They say that when they gathered up the tin, after having followed all the instructions, one of the pieces, the biggest, was in the shape—really the spitting image—of Christ on the cross. But you shouldn't pay too much attention to this, because it's always the same: give people a miracle, and they'll want to see two. In any case, they all slept soundly, without fear, and when they woke they all said they felt clean, as if newly baptized.

And indeed it all came true exactly as she'd foretold. She didn't want payment and wouldn't accept any gifts either. The worms started disappearing, and by the end of the two weeks not a single one remained. Admittedly by that time it was the middle of September, and the cooler air had come and chased away August's stifling heat. But that's a whole other theory.

The most curious thing of all is that if you ask any of the locals today, some will struggle to remember the episode before telling you it was actually no big deal. Others will deny ever having seen a white worm—whatever next; how absurd!

* * *

Along came water and put out the fire that burned the stick that killed the dog that ate the cat that ate the mouse that ate the cheese that was all the old woman and the old man had to eat.

Third Song
_____

THE HE-GOAT

He was the strangest-looking pilgrim they'd seen in years, though admittedly they hadn't seen that many lately. Long, dirty hair merging into the dirty beard; beard merging into the woolen poncho, so old that it looked like dragon skin or the bark of an oak tree, and so long that it reached his ankles. The mouth behind the beard was smiling like a strange mollusk. His voice was deep and smooth but his eyes were blue like a wolf's, and frightening, because they seemed to pierce right through you as if to speak to someone behind you, or possibly someone deep inside you. The del Molín woman's youngest burst out crying the second he saw him. Even the priest refused him sanctuary—"He can't be a pilgrim on his way to Santiago, he looks like a savage," he said, "or if he is heading there, it'll be because he's committed a lot of sins"—and the man had to go to Cobre to find a bed. They were saying that the previous night he'd slept in the cloisters at the church in Llamero, but now the sky was threatening snow. He simply wanted some space on the floor by the fireside, and rumor had it he could tell stories, plus he'd travelled round the world, but nobody dared invite him into their home. Finally, Margarita la de Cachín got rid of him by saying she had a sick little one in bed, and she suggested he try Cobre. She was probably thinking, rather spitefully, that someone who looked like a forest spirit would feel right at home in the house of a witch and a demon.

The dogs alerted them to his presence some time before he arrived, and Olegaria opened the top part of the door when he was little more than a dark spot coming along the road. Lino was five years old and was holding his mother's hand. It was already dark inside the house but quite the opposite outside. Though the light dazzled them at first, it didn't seem strong enough to illuminate the man's face, which looked like a carved totem. But his eyes were gleaming in their dark sockets, as if the pale evening light was emanating from them. He raised a hand in greeting, but it looked as if he were blessing them, like the Jesus in the wooden carving at the church. In the other, he was holding a staff made from a hazel branch, which must have only just been cut, since it was still white.

He said he'd been told that kind-hearted people lived here and that all he wanted was a roof over his head for the night. The clouds had a silvery glow because the gods had been polishing their treasures and the trees had lowered their branches to let the snow glide off, to prevent them from snapping under its heavy weight. Tomorrow at dawn he would be on his way, and there'd be nothing left of him but a story or two that would grow in their souls and one day protect them with their shade.

Wordlessly Lino's mother unbolted the door and opened it. They stepped aside to let him pass, but he stood on the threshold for a few seconds, hesitating, as if he were about to wade into an icy river. He sniffed the air and winced. He closed his eyes. He felt the warmth, smiled, and took a step forward. Then another. The man was moving as though he were much taller than he was, and bowed his head needlessly as he passed under the chestnut ceiling beams and through the doorways. He was moving as though he really were the giant that Lino would remember for the rest of his life.

Then he seemed to shrink as he sat down on a small wooden stool near the fire. Stretching his hands out close to the flames, he sat in silence for some time, watching the little fire through half-shut eyes, while Lino and his mother watched him in turn. He turned his gaze toward the kitchen, so pitiful that it didn't even have a cheap coal-fired stove, as one might expect. Instead, a pile of logs had been lit directly on the earth floor. His eyes swept over the twisted black poker, over a trivet with feet so warped you'd think the pot on top was full of stones rather than leftover cabbage stew, over a kneading trough that looked like the coffin of a child who'd starved to death, over the wooden bench, so worn down by tired lives that the seat was full of holes and didn't have a single corner remaining. Lino and his mother were sitting on the bench observing him—his dripping beard, his woolen poncho giving off steam as if it were a stain beginning to burn off, the bag down at his feet, which were shod in makeshift sandals of leather and esparto grass and socks made from a strange-looking material, a cross between wool and wood fern, almost certainly alive—as he observed everything around him. His gaze shifted from the bench and took in the pile of cooking pots, the black eye of the bread oven, the dark walls and the earth floor; but also the horseshoe nailed above the door, the cowbell engraved with a cross hanging from a nail on the wall, and the piles of dried bay, rue, and elder on the windowsill; the chopped-up deer antler; and the stag beetle antlers, which, even in the dim light, he could see glinting as if they were made from jet like the black hand that glinted at Olegaria's neck. Lastly, his eyes met theirs, and it didn't surprise them to find that his had turned green.

Olegaria served him some leftover stew and a glass of thick, flavorsome wine so dense that it stained your teeth red. He thanked her and ate hungrily and drank gratefully. No one could tell how old he was; Lino's mother, whom he remembered as having always been old, serene, and tired, like a poplar in a storm, was nineteen.

When he'd finished eating, he stroked his beard thoughtfully. He took a corn cob pipe, a roll of tobacco that smelled like a cemetery, and a piece of light-colored wood with a dark tip out of his bag. Next, he set light to a little twig in the fire and used it to light the pipe. Exhaling a mouthful of thick smoke, he picked up the piece of light-colored wood and pushed the tip into the fire until it began to glow. As he blew on the ember a light silky smoke filled the room with a sweet fragrance they'd never smelled before. The wooden beams in the ceiling creaked, and outside an animal let out an angry roar. Then he began.

He told them his name was Lugo and that he was a story-teller by trade. He said that since he had no house or village or country or wife or family, he was at home anywhere. He told them that, since he was never any good at hunting or growing crops or carving or coveting or earning money or learning one single profession, he'd chosen to pursue all of them at the same time. He told them that, since he'd never believed in God, not the Christian one, nor that of the Moors, nor that of the Chinese in China, nor that of the blacks in Africa, not even in the Devil, he'd decided to believe in all of them. He said he wanted to learn all the stories in the world so that he could tell them to whomsoever deserved to hear them, and live on in them forever.

He told them that stories are the voice of the spirits, and because of this they are eternal and can't just be made up. He told them that spirits are everywhere, in the trees, in the river, in the animals, also inside of us, and it is they who give life to things. He said that the evil spirits were those who weren't happy in the vessel they'd been assigned, and this was why they wanted to kill us, to expel the good spirits from our bodies and take their place. He told them that stories can appease the bad and cheer the good and remind them that everything, in the end, is a story. He told them that of all the spirits the worst were the ones inside flies, and that is why they were always buzzing in a mad frenzy around whatever was dying. He said you should never kick stones, because this is where the spirits that still hadn't found a vessel waited, and this was why you often found stones all piled up at crossroads, to trap the evil spirits so they wouldn't possess the passing travelers. And he told them that of all the spirits the best ones were the ones in trees, and because of this they shouldn't be cut down, or not unless it was absolutely necessary and we'd asked for their permission beforehand.

He told them that even though all this was true they shouldn't talk to anyone about it, as the evil spirits could use it against you and punish you by taking over your body. He said he'd known a decent woman in Pajares whom, a long time ago, they'd killed for talking about such things. He told them she was called Marichuloca and that she'd been accused of kidnapping children to look after her knots of toads. He told them her frightened spirit had taken refuge in an old tree trunk close by, and all that remained of this log was the little piece of white wood whose fragrance they were now smelling. He told them he'd been burning it for years, just as the people of Pajares had burned her, and that once he'd burned all of it, the sweet smoke would be able to find its way into a good tree.

He told them he was a storyteller. He said that stories were more important than anything and that they had to be protected to prevent evil spirits from sucking the life from the earth. He told them that all you had to do to hear the stories was pay attention; they were in books and in prayers, but also in the most trivial chatter, in the most mundane gossip, in an ordinary hello, in dreams at night and in silences. He said that they are a voice that is present, ever present for those who listen. He told them that this is the moment and that we have the voice, he told them that we have the time, we have all time.

* * *

Lino was the first to nod off, stretched out on the bench, with his head on his mother's lap. Then she fell asleep too. When they woke up a bright white light was streaming in through the window and the fire had burned itself out, leaving a tiny pile of ash. On the stool, they found a little black leather-bound book. A short while later the father arrived home. The bad weather had forced him to stay in the bar all night. His feet left tracks in the immaculate snow.

* * *

Isabel la de Ramona is known as Isabelina because her mother was Isabel, and even though her mother died thirty years ago, she'll always be the little one. Ramona was her great-great-grandmother, a very large and foul-mouthed woman from whom she inherited the family nickname, her overly broad shoulders, and her large size, rather too large for her diminutive. From her mother she inherited her first name and a liking for fantasy—she's even seen the ghoulish *Santa Compaña* lost souls and had a chat with them, although for some reason they didn't take her with them. Sometimes people call her Isabelina la Fantástica, to remind others not to take too seriously her claims that a mischievous *trasgu* goblin steals white sugar from her cupboard, or that on some nights the constellations change their shape to trick her, or that an angel sometimes watches over her from the foot of her bed.

It must be said that, at eighty, Isabelina has shrunk so much that her diminutive might be beginning to suit her. She's walking under her large umbrella, and her back is stooped. As the years pass, all living creatures gradually bend down toward the ground, as if the earth is constantly trying to tell them something and they can't hear it, because life makes us deaf to everything that isn't life. It's raining as if it's always been raining. The children are looking out at the street through the windows, their noses flat against the glass. The light inside the houses is yellow, as if all the light bulbs were low wattage. The encampment has become a quagmire where hundreds of mushrooms have sprung up. Big raindrops beat down on the huge canvas drum formed by the tents. The men are all turning back into apes, poking their heads out of their caves, with nothing to do but fear and dream. And the news is on hold, because news stories need either a lot of cold or a lot of sun to grow. Isabelina is carrying a large black umbrella and wearing heavy clogs; she can barely pick up her feet, and her dragging footsteps are echoing through the narrow street. This is the sound that makes the television reporter, fed up with recording the rain, notice the large elderly woman bent over like a weeping willow, and decide to ask her a few questions.

And Isabelina, unsurprisingly, comes out with a load of crazy nonsense.

She says that Marcelino is a saint. Not simply a good person, as the reporter first understood her to mean, but a true saint. She says his mother was one too, and cured many people, and everyone in the village knows it. His mother performed miracles, Isabelina says, and pauses, possibly realizing that she's built up too much momentum on the run-up and needs to figure out where she's going to land. But then she lets herself go and even clasps her big bony hands together in dramatic fashion, as if she were praying. And poor Marcelino has also performed miracles: with just one look, he cured her of the rheumatism that would have been the death of her. And everyone knows that when he was an altar boy he cured Don Alfredo's nephew of cancer simply by stroking his head. On top of that, the Virgin Mary would appear to him and his mother and talk to them and give them the strength to bear the torment his father, the Devil himself, inflicted on them. And not only the Virgin, but San Antonio too, who continues to watch over Marcelino now that his mother is dead, and has done so since he was a child, she says.

Isabelina la Fantástica isn't little, as her diminutive suggests, but she does live in a fantasy land, although only the villagers know this last fact. But the villagers always believe what people say on the television. Especially the old folk, who cannot imagine that these politicians, presenters, experts, and well-educated city folk could lie or even tell half-truths. If it's on TV, it must be true. And so, for once, they begin to think Isabelina might be telling the truth. As for Isabelina, she too believes everything she sees on TV, and is now absolutely convinced that what she's said is true, because so many people have taken her seriously.

* * *

There is something up there, and that is why children risk their lives attempting to climb to the tops of trees. They sail through a sea of green leaves in a living wooden boat. It is home, the original home, because it is the first place we were safe, and children with no memories remember it. It is a tower from which you can look into the future; you can see before you everything a human could possibly need.

There is something up there, for sure, and that is why Marcelino climbed up the great oak tree in the forgotten garden. From up there he could make out, beyond the mountains, the shape of the rocky white Cordillera Central. Then he looked northward, but he could only see the wooded valley, like two cupped hands ready to drink, with the river flowing through it. The thick branches of the hundred-year-old oak stretched skyward, inviting him to continue his ascent.

Hearing the caw of a crow, he looked up. He heard beating wings and saw a beautiful vulture taking off from one of the uppermost branches to attack a crow. Other crows came squawking to its assistance. The vulture was flying in tight circles and hurtling toward them. Although the crows were taunting and shrieking at it, the vulture was much stronger. Eventually they gave up and flew off. The vulture circled the tree a few more times and returned to its branch, where Marcelino spotted a nest, and in it a lone chick with whitish feathers, cheeping away happily.

Then it happened: the breeze caught some of the black feathers pulled out in the fight, carried them along, and let them float down onto Marcelino's shoulders and onto his head.

* * *

The first to arrive was a family of Peruvians who were living in Oviedo.

As they went in, the dark empty church echoed their footsteps. The music from the festival at the encampment could be heard faintly in the distance, getting louder whenever silence fell. Blackened by time and neglect, the virgins and the saints watched them approach the altar with surprise, like their ancestors who, hidden in the forest, watched the first Christians disembark on the beach. A creak sounded from the confessional booth as if someone were spying from behind the grille. The only three candles to have been lit flickered all alone in front of the Virgin, but they always did, because they had little bulbs that would light up if you put a coin in the slot. They paid their respects to Jesus Christ, kneeling to say an Our Father, although it wasn't him they'd come to see. Instead they were there for San Antonio, who, along with his faithful pig, had been resisting temptation since the eighteenth century in a side chapel. When the woman reached him she took several real candles out of her bag and lit them. The shadows fell away from the saint's face and his varnished wooden eyes shone with emotion at the warmth of the family's faith, the likes of which he hadn't felt in decades. Husband and wife knelt on the cold stone floor and began to pray. The stone walls echoed their prayers over and over until they sounded like a congregation.

They prayed for their youngest son, who was in the ICU burning up with a fever the doctors couldn't explain, like the burning bush that gave Moses his faith, like the way the woodpile would have burned, the one on which Abraham was prepared to sacrifice his only son to prove his love for God.

Their elder son, who was seven, waited for them in the little tree-lined square in front of the church. Even if he had been bored, he wouldn't have complained or pestered them, but he wasn't bored, because he was playing with some other children he'd met there, and time, which is light when you're playing, flew by. And he was having such a good time with his new friends that, two hours later, when his tired but serene-looking father came out to fetch him and told him to go in and pray for his brother to get better, the child was somewhat surprised, for he'd forgotten about his little brother and it felt as if all this had been part of some story that grew more and more horrible but just wouldn't end. Nevertheless, he did as he was told and entered the darkness of stone, wood, and wax. He knelt at his mother's side.

As they were leaving in silence, the child let go of his father's hand and retraced his steps. He took from his trouser pocket a small, green, badly bruised cider apple, which he'd picked up in the square, and he set it down beside the candles, in front of San Antonio. His parents were touched by this kind, innocent gesture.

That same night the fever disappeared, as quickly as it had come, and his little brother was out of danger.

The following Monday, San Antolín's priest was surprised to find several kilos of fruit in front of the altar, and at San Antonio's feet. Two weeks later, the church had begun to smell of fermented apple, like a cider factory, and they were gathering up several sackfuls of apples every morning.

* * *

Listen carefully: it sounds like the waves of a sea, a sea that's far away, or perhaps deep inside; like a breeze rippling feathers in a forest in summertime, or the babble of a river that has finally found its course after flowing idly for so long. You may well have heard it, most likely when you were children, but you've forgotten it because, like all truly important things, there is nothing, absolutely nothing to learn from it. Listen, the difference between a miracle and magic is that the first doesn't trick you; it never goes against the laws of nature, never creates anything that didn't already exist, never pulls a rabbit out of a hat, doesn't bestow the gift of flight, or make the visible invisible, or the small big, or the big small, or the weak mighty. Magic, on the other hand, is the product of anxieties and desires, and raises a thousand questions. The miracle is so simple that it always leaves you speechless.

We have the voice and we have the time. We have all time.

* * *

His father used to say that the Devil makes work for idle hands, and perhaps because he himself was a devil, he took it upon himself to ensure that Marcelino always had both hands full, practically from when the boy learned to walk.

Marcelino was only able to rest during the short time it took him to learn to pray before the priest kept his hands busy again. And later, after they'd both died, he didn't know how to stop. Because if you push something, it pushes something else in turn; and this, something else; and so on, forever. If you cut something, you have to cut a lot more, and cut again when it grows back. If you get up, you have to watch you don't fall. If you throw something down, you have to stop it coming back up. If you put up fences, you have to keep others out. If you own something, you have to protect it. If you put out a foot and let yourself fall forward, you have to put out the other foot and take another step and then another, until the end of your life, because walking is simply stopping yourself from falling at the last second. And yet for Marcelino those two weeks in the sanatorium, suspended between the old world and the new, both keeping one eye on him, without his axe or any other tool, without anything to do or even anything he could do, tired and a little hungry but warm, calm and with a bed to sleep in—those two weeks really were the best weeks of his life.

Every morning a robin with long feet, each like a single brushstroke of ink, would come to the windowsill to wake him. And what of the pure white cat lying in the tall grass, enjoying the sun, that didn't run away when Marcelino came near, and even let him stroke it? And what about the night he woke with a start thinking he could hear rats but instead found a tiny hedgehog eating his leftovers, a hedgehog who'd made his home in a little pile of dry wood in the corner of the room, and for whom he afterward left a small piece of bread every evening? And what can we say about the time a snake, its flank the color of a sunlit river, stopped still by the large rock where Marcelino was sitting, fixing him with its gaze, and then, with a flicker of its tongue, was gone? Heavens above! And a few days later he found the second shed skin of the year by the rock, a crystal sheath, a gift from the snake. Sitting on that same rock where, from that point on, he spent most of his time, his eyes became sensitive to the changes in the light produced by clouds passing in front of the sun, and the different shades of green of the fields, forest, and valley— opaque like a bottle of cider, transparent like a restful sleep, rich like a gem, dark like weariness—that shifted depending on the time and the wind. And what of that other wonderful morning, when he awoke covered in sawdust from wood-worms devouring a ceiling beam and the tiny specks of wood were glittering in the air like frankincense, like myrrh, like silver? What to say about all this? Isn't it better to say nothing at all?

* * *

Marcelino wasn't the first saint in the village, however. Long before he was born, Salustiano saw the Devil.

Salustiano was sixty years old and both his arms had been rendered useless by a quack doctor who cut through his tendons while attempting bloodletting to cure him of a fever. He was then unable to work in the fields with his sons, and masked the sorrow he felt at being a broken tool by drinking all day long. Salustiano wasn't violent and had never been a bad man; he wallowed in self-pity but didn't take it out on anyone else. From morning till night, he could be found propped up at the bar in Casa Ricardo with his tumbler of wine, his spindly arms gently folded as though he had an invisible baby in them, trying to catch someone's eye so that he could tell them how strong he used to be, how no one was better or quicker with a scythe, that even as a boy he'd worked as a day laborer in Galicia, and that because he'd earned so much money he'd been able to marry his wife. He was always the last to leave when they closed the bar, and he would walk home over a bridge, through a little wood, taking small steps, leaning every so often against a tree or against the stone wall of the bridge, muttering to himself in a never-ending conversation. Until one night, on that very bridge, the Devil appeared to him in the form of a giant hound that stood up on its hind legs to talk to him.

What the Devil said to him he didn't reveal, but the following day he climbed up to the top of the stilt granary beside his house and never came down. He never touched alcohol or felt sorry for himself ever again either.

His granddaughter Aurorina was only a little girl when this took place, but now that she'd passed the age he was when he died, not a day went by when she didn't think of him. She'd recall him sitting in a little wicker chair on the gallery of the old granary, gazing over the valley, a faint smile on his lips. And even toward the end, when thick cataracts had veiled his eyes, he would continue to gaze and smile at whatever it was that he alone could see. His skin, like his pupils, was as white as his hair. Whenever she was allowed to, she would take his food up to him. She felt safe up in the old granary, its massive wooden beams weathered like the bones of a beached whale—stilt granaries are gigantic puzzles with hundreds of years of history, constructed without a single nail—as if the old granary were a boat riding the waves of time, sailing out of the void to head back to the void, from her childhood to her old age, from where she was now remembering him, on her way, she thought, to the place where they'd meet again.

But Salustiano didn't perform miracles, not during his lifetime, or afterward. And though the wicker chair is still there in the granary, and often creaks at night as though someone were sitting in it, neither did he reappear, except in the memories of those who'd known him.

As usual, the television is on. And as usual, it's on mute, after weeks of inflicting its incessant noise. The silent images are thrown down on top of each other like the cards the regulars are now shuffling once again. Youngsters gesticulating, opening and closing their mouths without saying anything; the same old panoramic vistas of the valley and the encampment; Isabelina with her hands clasped in prayer; and the little church where they were all baptized, where they were married, and where they'll be given their final send-off, about to be flooded by a tide of people in an enormous queue for the entrance, hemmed in like cattle between the yellow barriers erected by the council. All so new yet already so old. The news is a vegetable grown in a greenhouse; it might look good to eat but is completely tasteless, and you'll have had enough of it after the first bite.

Pando is sitting on a stool by the window. He is ignoring the TV and the card players. Of all the meteorological phenomena, rain is the one that produces the greatest sense of continuity. It's rather like when we see the first daisies and, before we know it, the sky is full of swifts again. When it rains, it seems as though it's never stopped raining. We forget the days in between, we forget the sun, we forget the warmth: rain is a monologue being performed on repeat for thousands of years. This is why four days of rain seem never-ending, and why when the sun comes out Northerners have the look of just-freed hostages about them. This is the reason holiday-makers get so upset when it rains, because in the rain they can't shake off their past: rain is the past; rain is the family that makes you come home; rain is our unhappy childhood.

Nevertheless, some pilgrims love the rain. Pando sees them going past. Some are wearing walking boots and covered up with plastic capes they've bought from Ana la de Colorines, who's never had it so good. Some are even walking barefoot and not covered up at all, proving that their faith is stronger than the clouds, while at the same time atoning for their sins. They're walking the pilgrim's way from San Antolín to Lino's house, which they've divided into fourteen stages like the Way of the Cross. At the end of each of these, they kneel and pray before walking on.

Pando watches a lady walk up the hill dragging a shopping trolley protected by a sheet of clear plastic. It takes him a while to realize that what she's pulling isn't a trolley but a wheelchair in which a little boy is sitting. His body is twisted and his fists are clenched. Some kids at the next table see him too and are outraged. But Pando is like the forest-covered mountain and has seen all the trees grow twice over. This forest has seen such things before.

Like when Bernadina promised to crawl up to the Sanctuary of the El Fresno Virgin on her knees if her husband came back alive from the war, and the husband came back and she went up, resolute at the start, then hurting, bleeding, and in ecstasy at the end. Like when Pando himself had to wear a Nazarene's habit for a whole year, because a female neighbor had promised God that he would if her kid recovered from a cold, which wasn't even that bad—back then you could promise things on behalf of others without asking their permission, and they would have to fulfill the promise. When the year was up, he removed the tasseled silk cord from the purple tunic and carried on wearing it for a few years; he really did look rather good in it. Or like when the entire parish spent two weeks walking to Covadonga one summer, and halfway through the journey they put the little children on a train to get them there sooner because they were so tired. Or like when Manolo hanged himself from a linden tree and his tormented soul went roaming around, making the cows sick and the pigs skinny, causing havoc with the calving, ruining the harvests, until they organized a procession and all prayed for his soul for several days and nights and sent him to purgatory. Or like all the trips to Lourdes, in

France, which were so expensive that you had to save up for years or borrow from the gentry; or to Fátima in Portugal, slightly cheaper and closer but with such poor roads and such terrible food, and bedbugs in the beds, that it seemed like the end of the earth—all to do the same thing this lot are doing seventy years later. Or like the time Maruxa went to San Andrés de Teixido in Galicia because she couldn't get pregnant, and a month later, when she came back, she was. Pando smiled as he remembered the child, who'd been born earlier than expected but was a very big baby. Maruxa claimed it was a miracle, but from then on they all called him El Gallego, the Galician.

And El Gallego's son, Josín el Gallego, is flinging his card down onto the table. A cigar is hanging from his mouth, despite the notice stuck on the wall behind the bar which reads *No Smoking*. It's yellow from all the tobacco smoke.

A sudden gust of wind brings the rain lashing against the windowpanes. The TV flickers on in silence. Above the drumming rain, the conversations, and the sound of cards hitting the table, you can hear voices singing outside.

* * *

And Marcelino was sensing the birds' fear as night closed in; they were bidding farewell, as if the Sun were going out never to return, before falling silent.

And the fireflies flirting with the stars, returning part of their light to them.

And in the grass the glinting eyes of a fox, mesmerized by the fire.

And the cuckoo giving thanks for the coolness of the earth. And the frogs chirping and the toads croaking. And the crickets and the cicadas groaning, shrieking in pleasure before falling spent to the ground.

And the mice causing the wooden floor to creak as if great heavy men were walking on it. And the sound of the woodworm slowly working away. And the bats drawing Chinese characters around the fire.

And the smell of grass as, contentedly, it lies down to sleep. And the flowers closing because no one and nothing is there to see them now.

And the night that no longer leaves him exhausted, the night that is filled with sounds and smells, the night that is no longer his father.

And the Moon, full, white, serene, because she holds within her the nests where all the swifts sleep. The full Moon, like the Virgin with her arms cradling, only without the child.

* * *

Since his last cow died of old age two years ago, Ricardo now cuts the grass for no one in particular. Then, once it's dry, he burns it. You're not allowed bonfires during the summer, but country people don't take much notice of this, because with the amount it rains you'd be hard-pressed to set fire to the mountain. And so right across the little field there are mounds of grass slowly smoking, like great piles of strong-smelling cigar ash. It's a fresh and bitter scent that takes any Northerner back to their childhood. He's not the only one either, because here and there you can see little plumes of smoke rising up into the sky, and the whole valley appears to be veiled in a fine mist.

Ricardo takes a break and drives his pitchfork into the earth, like a warrior at the end of a battle. He remembers that when he was a child he used to think that the smoke from the bonfires was what blotted out the sky when it rained. People usually light the fires on particularly hot, sunny days, which are rare, so what usually happens is that the same night or the next day the sky clouds over. Confusing one type of vapor for another—say, clouds—is easy; and that's how magic is made. His grandfather, by the same logic, believed that the clouds were great sheep whose shepherd was a spirit called Nuberu.

The smoke isn't rising; it's being swept along the road instead. Two buses go past, one after the other, and chase it off to the sides of the road. Two of the many buses that arrive daily from all over. Ricardo doesn't know what they're coming for. His wife has told him that most of them come to leave gifts and offerings at the feet of San Antonio. She says they leave photos, wish lists, crucifixes, rosary beads, dolls, even pieces of wedding dresses, according to La Rumana, who now needs to go and clean the church every single day. And apparently some of them have been in Lino's house and taken everything. They have made crucifixes with the wood from the bed and cut up the sheets as though they were relics. And Juanín said it seems that the Virgin Mary, the one they used to pass around the village, was in Lino's house, and they must have taken that as well, because it turned up at the entrance to the iron mine where Lino had been hiding. You've got to be stark raving mad to lug that thing miles up into the mountains, Ricardo thinks. Beside Lino's house there's a wooden signpost with an arrow that reads "The Saint's Way." Now they're not only walking to Cobre, which is quite close by, but to the mine, to see the Virgin that everyone had forgotten existed.

Now the wind changes and blows the smoke into Ricardo's face; he coughs, waves his hands, and steps back. Then the smoke rises straight up to the sky, as if it's given up fighting. When night begins to fall, the little bonfires glow red from within. In the darkness they look like gigantic fireflies.

* * *

You see, our ideas aren't ours. They never have been. We've acquired our most profound beliefs without even realizing it. Your identity, the one you're ready to kill or die for, is a costume stitched together from a thousand rags and scraps.

Fear is real, not he who fears; death is real, not he who dies.

With any luck, every century or millennium, someone comes along with a new vision. Someone, somehow, has an idea no one has had before. Some will call this person a prophet; others, a madman, shaman, artist, or fool. But in every case this person, this first custodian of enlightenment, will pay very dearly, and when they eventually pass on, they'll become simply one part of this voice, a new tone, a harmony, a small grain of truth in which, believing it to be our own idea, we'll put our faith.

* * *

What year would it have been? That's right, it was 1940, because it was just after the civil war. In fact, that was why they were walking to the Virgin of Covadonga, passing through several Asturian parishes on the way: so that everyone could thank her for supporting the righteous Christians in their crusade to crush the atheist Reds. Something that happened then and hasn't happened since. The walking to the Virgin, we mean; the crushing keeps crushing away any chance it gets.

A statue of the Virgin Mary known as La Santina arrived in San Antolín in a truck the afternoon before the procession. The police escort that accompanied her was so big people started to wonder if General Franco himself had come too. She was kept in the church overnight.

It so happened that Sagrario had been picked as the *beatona*, or chosen one, of the village. This special honor meant that she was the one who cleaned the church, dusted the statues, changed the flowers, cleared away the used candles, and even performed the sacraments. Her devotion knew no bounds. It reached the point where some malicious people even began to suggest that she was the priest's mistress, but nobody believed it, because she was so ugly that she'd never been with a man, and so she remained an old maid, in both senses of the word.

She'd been going door to door for a year now, asking all the residents in the parish to donate money for a new mantle to present as a gift to the Virgin when she came. And because no one wanted to be seen as unchristian, she was able to afford one of the more expensive ones. It was vitally important to her, her last shot at booking her passage to Heaven and divine love, for on Earth she'd known nothing but loneliness and contempt.

The procession set off early in the morning. Along the route, the fields and verges were crowded with children and farmworkers cheering and shouting "Beautiful!" at the statue. Four police officers were carrying her on a platform on their shoulders, and behind them followed a long snake made up of hundreds of heads of slicked-back hair smelling of cheap cologne. Among them, and one of those closest to the Virgin, of course, was Sagrario. But she was looking sad and withdrawn, almost as if she were praying half-heartedly. And so that evening, Benjamina, who was very sharp and had spotted something was up, went to her house and asked her what was going on.

At first, Sagrario claimed it was nothing. But after the fourth glass of cherry anis, she burst into tears and confessed. "Oh, what have I done, what have I done?" she began. "Last night they brought La Santina and left her with us in the church. Don Servando and I dressed her in the new mantle. She looked so beautiful. The loveliest thing I'd ever seen. We prayed for everything to go well today, and then after praying we both went home. But I couldn't sleep. It's true, believe me. I was so nervous and I couldn't stop thinking that what I needed was to spend a little time alone with her. I don't know what came over me, but I couldn't get the thought out of my head. I started to believe it meant that she must be calling to me. So I got dressed and went back to the church in the early hours.

"She was so beautiful there in the candlelight, with her shining mantle, like a polished coin. I knelt and prayed and prayed. Then I begged her to help the needy. I must have been there for an hour, until I became so comfortable in her company that I began to feel sleepy. And I was on the way out, about to close the door, when—

"Oh, the shame!" cried Sagrario, and burst into tears again.

Benjamina comforted her, and given that by this point she would have cut off her own hand to know what had happened, she insisted that Sagrario tell her: she told her she was her friend and swore she wouldn't breathe a word to anyone. Even though the whole village knew what an old gossip Benjamina was, clearly Sagrario's urge to confess was stronger than her tendency to reticence, and she went on: "Oh, Heavens above . . . As I was on my way out, I turned back and looked on her in silence awhile. The skin of her hands, her dainty face, were so lovely, so white and pure, and her expression so kind that, and I don't know what came over me, the Devil made me . . . I thought it wouldn't do any harm to take a look under her dress. I was sure her body would be beautiful and her skin even whiter and purer. Oh, it's dreadful, just dreadful! But I went up to her and I lifted her dress and looked underneath . . . " Sagrario stopped, her eyes shining wildly, as if she'd had a vision. "There was nothing there!" she shrieked. "Absolutely nothing! Just two wooden poles nailed together in the shape of a cross, with the head and hands stuck on the ends! The Virgin is like one of those stick people children draw!"

Benjamina tried to console her, explaining that the most important thing was what the statue represented; the real Virgin Mary, not this stick one, was at God's side. But as soon as she was out of the door, she burst out laughing and didn't stop until she got home.

Sagrario never got over having committed this sinful act, let alone the crushing disappointment that came with it.

* * *

Along came a peasant and drank the water that put out the fire that burned the stick that killed the dog that ate the cat that ate the mouse that ate the cheese that was all the old woman and the old man had to eat.

* * *

And Marcelino saw the storm rolling down from high up on the ridge, making its way from valley to valley. And the first drops of rain, and the earth sighing as if kissed for the first time.

And a handful of rose petals dropped by the wind into the stagnant rainwater in the disused fountain.

And a fallen nest, like a lovesick scarecrow's heart.

And the gravel on the path in front of the steps, crunching underfoot like snow.

And waves of golden seeds floating in the air, shimmering in the August light.

And the tall grass turning yellow, dying in its plenitude.

And a black poplar tree heaving with sleeping magpies at nightfall.

And a piece of china, its edges rounded by time, sparkling on the riverbed, among the stones.

And the thousands of specks of light chasing each other through the green grass under a hazel tree.

And the dandelion clocks like old men's heads.

And the blackberries, all hot in the sun, and the ones in the shade, quite cool.

And the sun-drenched marble in the evening, warm as a puppy's belly.

And the perfect silence of moonless nights.

And the shooting stars tearing a ladder across the silk stocking of the night.

* * *

Let it be known that our sword was only ever made of wood and that our saints were but old statues that smelled of shit.

Take down the clocks and boast that you can control time.

Take down the rainbow, as if you could stop it from shining.

Take down the stars and throw them into the sea.

Take down the words and impale them on spikes, on the city walls, and at crossroads, to frighten the artists and poets.

Take down drama, the universe, and religion, and pave the great avenues of Progress with the rubble.

Set down your iron buildings that reach the sky. Set down your glass and iron buildings on top of the cathedral, which was built on top of the Romanesque church, which was founded on top of the Roman temple, which was built on top of the standing stones where animals were sacrificed to appease the same gods.

Inside these walls, you'll be safe.

Inside these walls, you'll be safe from the monsters you've created.

* * *

Marcelino's cart was traveling slowly along the road while in the sky the Great Bear's cart was moving off too. It was filled to the brim with straw and some of it was getting caught in the overhanging branches, like streamers at a fiesta. The sky was still clear, dazzlingly bright, but the valley had filled with blackness as though the night were welling up out of the ground, and the first bright stars were clinging on tightly in the sky. He could see the kitchen window in the distance, like a homely, yellow star.

It was half past ten when Marcelino arrived home. He could smell the stew his mother was cooking, its aroma mingling with the scent of the grass, bay, and rosemary that grew beside the road.

He washed his hands, splashed his face. He was twenty years old but went to his mother for a kiss, as he always did. Afterward he sat at the table waiting for dinner to be served. These two or three hours, while his father was in the bar drinking, were his only home. The gurgle of the pot simmering away, the warmth, the yellowish glow from the ceiling bulb, and knowing everything was all right, even if only for a brief time, allowed his mind to drift as he gazed out of the window. The streetlamps way down below in San Antolín lit up like a cluster of orange stars. Then the one in front of his house flickered briefly as the darkness reached it, and lit up too. Immediately, two little bats swooped out of the darkness and launched into an acrobatic display inside its sphere of light.

* * *

It was a night very much like that one, and it was summer too. When they told him to come, and set off toward the church, he was afraid that they were going to see the priest. They climbed the hill and sat under the arches by the entrance to the church. You could see the entire village from there—a string of colored bulbs lit up the field by the river where the fiesta was taking place that year. The oldest, a prepubescent kid with a beret and a big bulbous nose, took out a little packet and dished out cigarettes to all the others, some as young as seven. Lino was ten. The tobacco was coarse and black, rolled in thick paper without a filter. They smoked in silence. The music from the open-air dance reached their ears in muffled waves as if it were a memory. One of them took out some firecrackers and some of them began to jump about with excitement, but the older one said that was for kids, and it was time to do what they'd come for, and they calmed down.

Within the church grounds there was a tall streetlamp next to a white wall, which attracted moths and mosquitoes from all over the valley and consequently was also teeming with the bats that came to feed on the insects.

The children moved closer to the light and took some flat pieces of wood out of their pockets. They began to throw them into the air again and again. For a good while they stood there, playing this strange game, which Lino didn't understand, until one of them shouted out excitedly. They crowded around the little bat, which was still alive. Its radar had confused the piece of wood with a large insect and it had tried to catch it. The oldest boy held the bat in one hand and with the other stretched out its wings, repeating this several times so they could all see. Then he lit another cigarette.

"Look, Lino," he said, and the others moved out of the way to let him get a better view.

Not even they knew why they kept on inviting Lino to join in their games. Perhaps to have a more innocent witness. The oldest boy brought the lit cigarette to the tiny animal's mouth; it bit on it desperately. The tip glowed several times.

"Look, look, it's smoking." And they all started cackling like little devils.

But that wasn't the endgame.

Lastly, they released the bat, which flew off, scared witless. It flew around in a circle several times, utterly confused, and smashed into the wall, to more cackling laughter. The bat was still strong enough and terrified enough to take off into the air again. But the next time it hit the wall so violently that it ruptured, leaving a red stain, a bloody brushstroke on the white canvas of the wall. Its body fell to the ground like an umbrella broken by the wind.

* * *

He was woken by his mother calling from the window for his brother to come for dinner. His brother wasn't answering, so she asked Lino to fetch him.

Lino went to the cowsheds, but he wasn't there. He looked in the hayloft, where he'd sometimes found him sleeping peacefully, exhausted after a day of hard playing, and he wasn't there either. He wasn't in the grain store, he wasn't hiding under the cart. He wasn't in the pigsty either, of course. He looked in the chicken coop. He looked by the woodpile. He wasn't in the sand heap under the chestnut tree, where he used to play at making buildings and roads.

He finally found him beside the rabbit hutch. He was squatting, completely absorbed, studying something in the palm of his hand. Lino didn't have time to see the treasure properly before his brother hid it, but it could have been two black marbles, a handful of blueberries or a few blackberries, or maybe some shiny-shelled crickets.

* * *

He must have been feeling very relaxed for them to have taken him by surprise like that. He'd been fishing in the river and a still-twitching trout hung from his hand, his fingers sunk into its gills.

They shouted, "Don't shoot!" and emerged from the bush with their rifles pointing toward the ground. There were four of them: three men and a lad of about fifteen. Marcelino didn't try to escape, he stood where he was, calmly, in silence, and the hunters surrounded him. Luckily, none of them was his brother.

The one who seemed to be in charge, a man of about sixty with brown skin, white hair, a long graying beard, and blue eyes, moved away a little, and the others followed. The young lad, who had several dead quails hanging from his shoulder, stayed close to Marcelino. A short time passed as the others talked. The older one was moving his hands gently, as if he were patting a well-behaved dog on the back. Then they came back to form a circle around Marcelino, who was waiting, breathing heavily but calmly, like a just-broken horse.

"Marcelino, you must get out of here," said the white-haired one. "We were stopped by several police officers back that way. They can't be far behind us. They'll be here today or possibly tomorrow."

He looked at Marcelino intently, smiling a little, as if he still couldn't believe they'd stumbled across him. Marcelino's skin was covered in dirt, his clothes were now a bundle of rags, his hair was black and his beard red, almost blond around the mouth; his eyes were small and shiny; his eyebrows were as bushy as chestnut husks. A wood pigeon in a nearby tree cooed, breaking the spell.

"Don't use the tracks and don't head up the mountain. You're better off following the river downstream. They're not as likely to look for you in that direction," he explained. "But you can't stay here. You've got to go."

Next, he signaled to the boy to come, and took the bundle of quails from him. He offered the bundle to Marcelino, who didn't move. The man stepped even closer, took hold of Marcelino's right hand and gently opened it. He placed the end of the string inside and closed it. Again the man smiled. Once more he called the lad to him, lifting the rucksack off his back before setting it down in front of Marcelino. "Take this as well: there are matches, firelighters, a first aid kit, a lamp, and a knife."

Lastly, he took off his jacket and put it round Marcelino's shoulders. The man and his friends couldn't help smiling: something about Marcelino standing there made them think of a little boy dressed up in clothes he'd taken from his parents' wardrobe.

* * *

Marcelino remained motionless for some time, until the sound of their footsteps in the undergrowth had petered out. Like a hedgehog that had rolled itself into a ball on sensing danger, he finally uncurled and made a run for it. The first man reminded him of his brother. Or rather the man his brother should have become. It was the first time in his entire life that anyone except his mother had given him a present.

* * *

When night fell and nature lay down to sleep tired and satisfied, like a young woman after making love to her sweetheart for the first time, Marcelino began his descent, following the course of the stream.

When the stream flowed into the Neva, as calm and black as night itself, he stepped out onto the bank and gazed at the thousands of campfires and bonfires glowing in the distance, like armies of heathens bearing down on him to reclaim what was rightfully theirs; as if the stars were a flock of geese that had broken their journey to rest for the night in the valley. He couldn't have known, of course, that they were the lights from the huge encampment and from San Antolín itself, burning in a great blaze of theater, politics, and religion.

He listened closely: deep drumbeats and all kinds of music, jumbled together, and dogs barking; a constant rumble, almost a roar, like a furious sea; disembodied shouts carried on the wind; robotic amplified voices rendered incomprehensible by the reverberation. The crickets and other animals around him were silent, as if they weren't there at all, or as if they too were trying to understand what was happening. What was happening... How can you know, when it's impossible to know anything, when everything's underway and, however much they try, no one can explain anything anymore?

Marcelino kept on heading downstream. He waded into the river again. It was deep, but at least he would be safe from those fires. He'd be able to cut straight through them.

* * *

They'd met a few months earlier, at university. He wasn't handsome but he wasn't ugly either, neither clever nor stupid, but he had personality and was sure of himself. She always spoke her mind, a trait she confused with sensitivity, but it didn't really matter because she was a sweet girl and much better-looking than him. Let's simply say that they were nice kids and they thought they were masters of their own destiny. That will do.

Still in the first flush of romance, they wanted only to nurture their love, so they'd gone for a walk, some distance from the camping area. They were fed up with the racket, which made it impossible for them, or anyone else, to bask in their passion. Hand in hand, they walked under the stars. As the boom of the fiesta gradually dimmed, the chirping of crickets and the croaking of toads grew louder. The smell of damp earth, manure, and dry grass went to their heads and made them believe that they were, perhaps for the first time, exactly where they wanted to be.

A couple of miles from San Antolín—letting themselves be carried away by that well-meaning but mediocre script-writer who whispers directions in lovers' ears—they left the path and went into a field overlooking the river. They lay down on the grass and looked up at the stars with that half-demented smile you get from too much moongazing.

Soon they were naked and panting. All the beings in the universe fell silent in wonder. Even the river turned down the volume on its babbling. His feet dug into the earth, pulling out clods. The scratches from the prickly wet leaves felt like caresses on her back.

Covered in life and dew, they lay next to each other holding hands. He lit a cigarette. She said: "I love you."

It was then, as the spell was lifting and their hearts were beginning to slow, and they'd begun to shiver, that they saw the man. At first, they thought it was just a branch moving, and they laughed at their own fear. But then they felt the unmistakable vibration of human eyes on them.

The boy jumped to his feet, trying to work out what to use as a weapon, his mind whirring through possible scenarios of this story of love in the wilderness turning into one of murder in the country or redneck rapists. "Hey, you prick! What the hell are you doing?" he shouted, pulling up his trousers and managing to sound threatening despite the slight tremble in his voice.

Marcelino came out of the shadows and showed himself in the milky-white moonlight. He had the pistol in his hand because he'd been there since before they arrived and they'd given him a fright.

"All right buddy, take it easy. It's okay, we're going now. We don't want any trouble," said the boy, feeling like this sentence, this scene, this entire thing was happening to someone else, who looked like him but wasn't him at all.

The girl stood up and put her arms around him, sobbing gently.

Marcelino came closer, and they could see his face. He was frowning, as if something was troubling him. But he didn't look threatening.

"Fuck, it's you, you ... you're Marcelino," said the boy. "Man, we've come here to support you. There are loads of us. From all over. Yeah. We're with you. All of us," he added clumsily, but stopped when his eyes came to rest on the pistol pointed at him.

They stood in silence. A whitish vapor was coming out of their mouths, as if the temperature had suddenly dropped. The girl shivered. Her naked body gleamed in his arms, his skin a little darker.

And then Marcelino spoke: "He didn't . . . he didn't hurt you?" he asked. "Do you . . . do you love . . . Do you love him? Do you? Do you love him?"

She didn't know how to answer this strange and unexpected question.

"You do love him, don't you?" Marcelino insisted, almost pleading.

"Yes. I love him," she said. "I love him very much."

Marcelino reached out and, as if he were a child touching the head of a newborn baby, stroked her breast. She felt the rough skin of his hand and flinched, but she wasn't afraid. Marcelino gazed at the palm of his hand, perhaps expecting to see the golden dust a butterfly leaves on your skin when you touch it. His face relaxed, his frown disappeared.

Then Marcelino smiled.

The young couple held their breath.

Without another word, Marcelino turned and began to walk toward the river. They stood in silence, watching him move away.

* * *

They were just a boy and a girl, not particularly significant individually, but an important part of this legend. We should also say that she wasn't lying and she truly did love him. And he her. They called their first child Marcelino.

* * *

He got up before the last stars had disappeared from the sky and went to milk the cows as he did every day. His mother was already there, busy doing something. As soon as he arrived, she took his hand and led him away from the cowshed. She brought him to the rabbit hutch, a large wood and wire box, which had been placed directly on the ground. "Look, Lino," she said.

There was nothing to see. The rabbits were silent, awaiting their impending death uncomplainingly.

"Look properly, Lino," his mother insisted.

The pale gray light of dawn was shining in his eyes and he couldn't quite make out what it was. He had to crouch down to see. Their black eyes, with their off-puttingly human eyelashes, were still black.

But they weren't eyes any more.

They were holes.

The rabbits were strangely calm.

"I saw it earlier, when I came to feed them."

The blind rabbits remained silent, chewing on the fat carrot of their pain.

Lino remembered the black marbles his brother had been holding in his hand the previous night.

"Do you think it was him?" his mother asked eventually, as if she could read his mind.

Lino shook his head.

* * *

The rabbits with their shining wet eyes like jet beads. The rabbits with their black eyes and their human eyelashes.

And his father, with his dark eyes like cigar stubs, and his face red with rage, shouting: "Look what your spells have done, bitch! One son a retard, and this one a psycho!"

And his father's fist—stone, night, death, pit—exploding against his mother's face. His mother sprawled on the floor, trying to defend herself against the blows.

And his brother crying, clinging to his father's leg, grabbing hold of his hoof, begging him to stop. And the father's fist—tomb, womb, oblivion, skull—hitting his brother's little face for the first time, the blood welling up like a new spring, the father goring, ready to kill every last one of his cubs. And Marcelino, with no choice but to attack, piercing his father's chest with his great young horns over and over. Until his father stops kicking. Until his father can punch no more. Until his father lies still, placid, as if sleeping, on the ground. At last, his hand open—valley, flower, lake, nest, treetop, summer—tightly clenched no more.

* * *

Nobody ever investigated and the doctor said he'd died of a heart attack or some such thing, since nobody had expected him to live much longer anyway.

* * *

They buried him in a small niche in the parish cemetery. The whole village turned out, but nobody looked upset.

His brother was the only one crying.

* * *

Just as he began to feel that he could go no further, the soft glow of daybreak took Marcelino by surprise. He was wet through and weak. The river was too deep and he walked alongside it, following the leaden waters, over the dunes and heathland of the floodplain. He thought it was snow, but when he crouched down he found that it was sand trickling through his fingers. He noted the deep smell of salt and the moist, cool breeze. He heard shrieks that reminded him of a baby crying, and tilted his head back to watch the gulls soaring above him in the gray sky. This world was not the Old World, neither the before, nor the present. This was an entirely undiscovered world.

Then, all of a sudden, when he reached the top of a dune, there it was in front of him.

The story goes that the first time Alfonso el del Rusco saw the sea he burst into tears, not because he was overcome by its beauty, but because he was imagining what a wonderful meadow it would have been if all this salty water hadn't ruined it. Alfonso was very old and beyond saving. Marcelino, on the other hand, sat down on the sand and took it all in. The arrows of his eyes had never reached distances such as these. He had never peered into an abyss such as this, except perhaps for the sky.

It was low tide and the sea had retreated like a sheet slipping off the bed in the morning, forming flat, tranquil pools; immense mirrors reflecting the silhouette—silvery like a fish's back—of sunrise.

The waves wearing away the world. The roar of the earth pouring itself into the water like a gigantic hourglass. The earth's curvature, like a bookshelf lightly warped under the great weight of its books. And on the horizon, way over there, a break, a huge dazzling rip in the pale gray fabric of the sky. First a glint of metal. Then an eruption. The axe blow cleaves the sky, splinters the remains of the night, and scares away the overconfident clouds, which carry on fighting even as they retreat. The volcano. He felt the heat of the sun's rays on his face, the breeze caressing his hair. He felt his heart beating, his breathing beating, his life beating. He felt the satiated emptiness, he felt silence.

A swollen sea without waves.

A fast-flowing river without banks or bed.

He took off his clothes at the water's edge. The little waves licked at his feet like lambs' tongues and bubbled around his ankles. He was on the very edge of the world, further out than anyone had ever been. The water reached his waist. A wave crashed over him, and a few seconds later he re-emerged clean, smiling.

Marcelino contemplates the world with newborn eyes. The great mountain range in the background, its peaks hidden in the clouds, crammed together with nowhere to go, like logs and branches swept by the river into a dam. The peaks all in a line, according to height or order of formation. The mountains, covered in a moss of forest; the night, hunkered down in their valleys before seeping into the ground.

The day, the light, are already here. They are here now, at last, the father and the mother, who are one. The he-goat in love with the girl. And the dazzling sea, as white as the girl's skin last night. And he, Marcelino, in the middle of all this. He, spectator and author. He, Lino: semen, son, fear, and love.

He knows what he must do. He holds his breath. Hanged men ejaculate for the last time; he for the first.

At last, the little stream flows into the sea.

When, hours later, his brother appears, with hundreds of people, Marcelino is no longer afraid. He hands himself over to him.

* * *

The cameras are recording when the police put him in a van. There are armed men. There are people in swimsuits, watching. There are people in swimsuits taking photos on their phones. Reporters are shouting to him. Youngsters are shouting. Some are clapping. Some are probably praying. He's handcuffed. But we can all see that he's smiling. He's smiling.

* * *

"And it was me he wanted, he came and he wanted me, whom no one loved and who had nothing.

"I was to marry my uncle the shoemaker, whom I'd never met, who didn't have a penny but still had more than us and lived in the capital.

"My father had arranged it with his brother when I was a little girl, and I always thought that was how it would be. But then, one day, I met him, or he met me. The he-goat. Back then, of course, I was innocent and pure and I didn't know who he was.

"I was just fourteen.

"It was my first *romería* festival.

"I was so excited that I'd get to see so many new people. It was the first time I'd been out of Cuanxú, where I never saw anyone apart from my poor parents, four neighbors and their children, two lads who'd left when I was little, the priest who changed year after year, occasionally the police, and two very old day laborers who could barely manage to cut the grass in exchange for a plate of terrible food and a few roast chestnuts.

"I put on a new dress, we left early in the morning, and I walked all the way to San Antolín with my mother. We were going because one of her sisters had taken ill and was dying and we went to say farewell. But it was also the time of the fiesta, and we had to go, because, though I didn't know it then, he was waiting for me there."

* * *

"When we arrived, it turned out that my mother's sister wasn't going to die after all, at least not yet, but there hadn't been time to let us know. My mother was delighted and the sister was delighted and her daughter too, because it was the *romería* and now her mother wasn't dying she could go without feeling guilty, and with something to celebrate. And I was delighted because now I didn't have to bid farewell to my mother's sister and my mother said you're old enough now to go to the *romería* and I was so happy and nervous about meeting so many new people. And my mother said *But don't be home late*, and my cousin said *Yes of course, woman, I'll look after her, yes she's good-looking but she seems smart enough and no one will take advantage of her*, and I painted my lips and eyes and off I went to meet him."

* * *

"On the way to the *romería* there was a rosemary bush and I sniffed a sprig and broke off a sprig and put it in my pocket to sniff when I wanted to ward off the evil eye.

"On the way to the *romería* there were chestnut and elm trees, and sun and birds and joy, and people carrying baskets and singing, and hampers filled with food that smelled of something that lasts forever and never goes bad.

"On the way, there was a big river, the biggest river I'd ever seen, and in it there were trout and salmon, which I thought were very big trout because I'd never seen salmon, and the water—rushing over the rocks and against the pillars of the bridge, the same water I peered into to see trout and big trout—was singing, like some of the people walking along bearing food and joy. On the way, there were eucalyptus and other trees I didn't know, like, I didn't know why they were so tall or why their tops were so far away or what smell it was that smelled like hunger and saintliness. On the way, we wore our wooden clogs and carried our shoes so that we could put them on when we got there and we'd be asked to dance, and I didn't know how to dance, but my cousin said don't worry I'll teach you and you just let him lead. On the way, the girls were looking at me and asking my cousin who I was and my cousin said I was her cousin from Cuanxú and that it was my first *romería* and they all laughed and I did too. On the way the boys, and among the boys, him. I didn't see him. But he saw me and he liked me."

* * *

"And when we arrived there were more people and families sitting in the meadow gathered around large picnic blankets, drinking cider and enjoying themselves. And children who were running and chasing each other and little tents and stalls selling sugarloaf and sweet chestnuts and aniseed cigarettes. And a wooden stage built from freshly cut branches, with braided garlands. And in the middle of the meadow a post, and—nobody knew why yet— cables strung with light bulbs suspended from them. And men at a very long wooden table drinking cider, and slapping each other on the back, and roaring with laughter and smoking, and their smoke curled upward in spirals until it caught in the hair of the girl they liked."

* * *

"And we sat ourselves down around a picnic rug with my cousin's friends, pressing our knees firmly together so as not to show our petticoats—not that I had one, but it was what you had to do—and they were cheerfully glancing over at the boys and laughing loudly at jokes no one had made, and the laughter was lifting up over their heads and floating through the air and falling softly onto the shoulder of the boy they liked."

* * *

"And then the band began to play, and what they were playing was lovely, and if I could I would have stayed there forever, listening and watching people, but my cousin said *Come on girl, up you get, come.* And some couples began to dance and then more began to dance, so beautifully they looked like long grass moving gently in the breeze. And a boy asked my cousin to dance and I was happy for her because she was happy. And another boy asked me to dance and I held his shoulders and spun and spun and carried on spinning among the other people spinning and we didn't even bump into each other once."

* * *

"The he-goat didn't have his balls out and I couldn't see his curly horns. And so when he saw me dancing with the other boy, he came up to us at the end of the song and said something to him that made him leave. And the he-goat smiled and offered me his hand and asked me very politely if I'd dance with him. And I, at fourteen years old, and knowing nothing, said yes. And it was me he had come for and he wanted me, whom no one loved and who had nothing."

* * *

"On the way back, the cool night and the tiredness that fell like drizzle over everything, and the joy of a sun-drenched flower as it closes its petals.

"On the way back, families laughing, worn-out little children asleep on their mothers' shoulders, empty baskets.

"On the way back, the crickets and the toads by the river. On the way back, the pairs of lovers lagging behind, walking more slowly, stretching time with two steps forward, one step back. On the way, my cousin left the path with a boy and that was the last I saw of her. On the way, just him and I, and he took my hand and I let him take it. On the way, he said I was beautiful and stroked a strand of my hair. On the way back, there on the road in front of my house, he kissed my cheek like someone drinking from a fountain. And I liked it because his breath smelled of fermented apple and chestnut leaves and of freshly cut wood and of fertile earth, and it was the first time a man had pollinated my skin."

* * *

"It was a week before he came to see me. He arrived on horseback one morning and he hadn't slept as he'd travelled through the night. He brought gifts: bottles of anis and cured meats. My father went out to greet him and my mother came toward me, smiling. He got down from his horse and my father said something very serious to him to which he gave a very serious answer, and they shook hands. Then I came out of the house, and I was quiet when we went for a walk together.

"He told me I looked very pretty in that dress, and I didn't tell him that he'd already seen it because it was the only one I had and I'd worn it at the *romería*, but even so I was pleased he said it because I believed it was true.

"He told me he'd buy me many more dresses, that he was rich and that he could take me away from here, and I said nothing.

"He told me I could have whatever I wanted and I didn't say anything at all. He told me things and I said nothing, because I was enjoying finding out about everything I hadn't known I could want.

"But he didn't notice the oak tree or the stream that were my oak tree and my stream. He didn't notice anything. But I liked him because he noticed me, and I still hadn't understood that he was only noticing me so that he could better notice himself.

"Before he left he kissed my cheek again, and this time his lips felt rougher and my skin was still burning the next day."

* * *

"He came to see me five more times, to tell me things and kiss me, until one day when he came not in the morning but at nightfall, and it wasn't to see me. My mother waited with me while he and my father talked on the hearth, where I couldn't hear them. Two hours later my father came and told me to go to him, and I went and there he was. There was an empty bottle of anis, and the remnants of some chorizo on a plate, and he wasn't smiling or saying anything and the fire was reflected in his eyes, like red embers at the bottom of a pit.

"*Daughter, you're to marry him*, my father said, and embraced me.

"And I married him.

"And I married him three weeks later. In the church at San Antolín. Just a few guests and fewer still for the meal. My father told him *I'm entrusting you with what I love most*, and then he took me. As soon as night fell, we went to his house, which was now our house.

"There I put on my nightgown and climbed onto the bed, waiting for him to put himself inside me.

"He sat on the edge of the bed and watched me tremble. He caught hold of a strand of my hair between his fingers and looked at it as if it were a flower. He smiled, for the first time that whole day, and then, a moment later, slapped me across the face as hard as he could.

"*So you know who's in charge around here*, he said.

"It was then that I saw those damaging horns for the first time. It was then that I saw those damaging, searing, great balls. And it was then that I wept, and while I was weeping he climbed on top of me and pushed himself inside me. His eyes were gleaming like a scarab beetle's shell. A swarm of angry flies was buzzing around us.

"That night was the beginning of hell and of joy.

"That night I became pregnant, son.

"And you came, and I who had nothing and no one to love, loved you."

* * *

We are the first words. We've been here before yet we've only just arrived. We are fiesta days and working days and dog days. We are the one who sets you alight and the one who puts out the flame. We are the one who wakes you in the morning and the one who leaves you shattered in your bed at night. Naturally, we are the one who then steals your sleep. We are the enemy and the only solace. A whisper. A fistful of words, the last words.

* * *

Along came a bear and ate the man who drank the water that put out the fire that burned the stick that killed the dog that ate the cat that ate the mouse that ate the cheese that was all the old woman and the old man had to eat.

"Ah, dammit, I'm lost. Where was I, man?"

"The bear, you got to the bear."

"Then, you greedy ass, I'll stop there."

MANUEL ASTUR is a Spanish author and journalist selected as "One of the Ten Most Interesting New Voices in Europe" by the European Union. He has written novels and collections of short stories and poetry and teaches literature at the Escuela de Letras de Gijón.

CLAIRE WADIE has a Masters in Translation from the University of Bristol and won the Peirene Stevns Translation Prize for *Of Saints and Miracles* by Manuel Astur.

DISTANT FATHERS
BY MARINA JARRE

This singular autobiography unfurls from the author's native Latvia during the 1920s and '30s and expands southward to the Italian countryside. In distinctive writing as poetic as it is precise, Marina Jarre depicts an exceptionally multinational and complicated family. This memoir probes questions of time, language, womanhood, belonging and estrangement, while asking what homeland can be for those who have none, or many more than one.

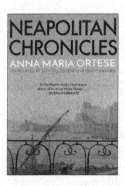

NEAPOLITAN CHRONICLES
BY ANNA MARIA ORTESE

A classic of European literature, this superb collection of fiction and reportage is set in Italy's most vibrant and turbulent metropolis—Naples—in the immediate aftermath of World War Two. These writings helped inspire Elena Ferrante's best-selling novels and she has expressed deep admiration for Ortese.

UNTRACEABLE
BY SERGEI LEBEDEV

An extraordinary Russian novel about poisons of all kinds: physical, moral and political. Professor Kalitin is a ruthless, narcissistic chemist who has developed an untraceable lethal poison called Neophyte while working in a secret city on an island in the Russian far east. When the Soviet Union collapses, he defects to the West in a riveting tale through which Lebedev probes the ethical responsibilities of scientists providing modern tyrants with ever newer instruments of retribution and control.

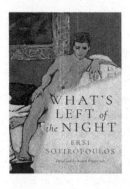

What's Left of the Night
by Ersi Sotiropoulos

Constantine Cavafy arrives in Paris in 1897 on a trip that will deeply shape his future and push him toward his poetic inclination. With this lyrical novel, tinged with an hallucinatory eroticism that unfolds over three unforgettable days, celebrated Greek author Ersi Sotiropoulos depicts Cavafy in the midst of a journey of self-discovery across a continent on the brink of massive change. A stunning portrait of a budding author—before he became C.P. Cavafy, one of the 20th century's greatest poets—that illuminates the complex relationship of art, life, and the erotic desires that trigger creativity.

The 6:41 to Paris
by Jean-Philippe Blondel

Cécile, a stylish 47-year-old, has spent the weekend visiting her parents outside Paris. By Monday morning, she's exhausted. These trips back home are stressful and she settles into a train compartment with an empty seat beside her. But it's soon occupied by a man she recognizes as Philippe Leduc, with whom she had a passionate affair that ended in her brutal humiliation 30 years ago. In the fraught hour and a half that ensues, Cécile and Philippe hurtle towards the French capital in a psychological thriller about the pain and promise of past romance.

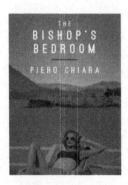

The Bishop's Bedroom
by Piero Chiara

World War Two has just come to an end and there's a yearning for renewal. A man in his thirties is sailing on Lake Maggiore in northern Italy, hoping to put off the inevitable return to work. Dropping anchor in a small, fashionable port, he meets the enigmatic owner of a nearby villa. The two form an uneasy bond, recognizing in each other a shared taste for idling and erotic adventure. A sultry, stylish psychological thriller executed with supreme literary finesse.

THE EYE
BY PHILIPPE COSTAMAGNA

It's a rare and secret profession, comprising a few dozen people around the world equipped with a mysterious mixture of knowledge and innate sensibility. Summoned to Swiss bank vaults, Fifth Avenue apartments, and Tokyo storerooms, they are entrusted by collectors, dealers, and museums to decide if a coveted picture is real or fake and to determine if it was painted by Leonardo da Vinci or Raphael. *The Eye* lifts the veil on the rarified world of connoisseurs devoted to the authentication and discovery of Old Master artworks.

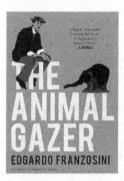

THE ANIMAL GAZER
BY EDGARDO FRANZOSINI

A hypnotic novel inspired by the strange and fascinating life of sculptor Rembrandt Bugatti, brother of the fabled automaker. Bugatti obsessively observes and sculpts the baboons, giraffes, and panthers in European zoos, finding empathy with their plight and identifying with their life in captivity. Rembrandt Bugatti's work, now being rediscovered, is displayed in major art museums around the world and routinely fetches large sums at auction. Edgardo Franzosini recreates the young artist's life with intense lyricism, passion, and sensitivity.

ALLMEN AND THE DRAGONFLIES
BY MARTIN SUTER

Johann Friedrich von Allmen has exhausted his family fortune by living in Old World grandeur despite present-day financial constraints. Forced to downscale, Allmen inhabits the garden house of his former Zurich estate, attended by his Guatemalan butler, Carlos. This is the first of a series of humorous, fast-paced detective novels devoted to a memorable gentleman thief. A thrilling art heist escapade infused with European high culture and luxury that doesn't shy away from the darker side of human nature.

THE MADELEINE PROJECT
BY CLARA BEAUDOUX

A young woman moves into a Paris apartment and discovers a storage room filled with the belongings of the previous owner, a certain Madeleine who died in her late nineties, and whose treasured possessions nobody seems to want. In an audacious act of journalism driven by personal curiosity and humane tenderness, Clara Beaudoux embarks on *The Madeleine Project*, documenting what she finds on Twitter with text and photographs, introducing the world to an unsung 20th century figure.

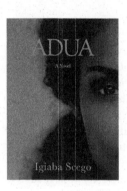

ADUA
BY IGIABA SCEGO

Adua, an immigrant from Somalia to Italy, has lived in Rome for nearly forty years. She came seeking freedom from a strict father and an oppressive regime, but her dreams of film stardom ended in shame. Now that the civil war in Somalia is over, her homeland calls her. She must decide whether to return and reclaim her inheritance, but also how to take charge of her own story and build a future.

IF VENICE DIES
BY SALVATORE SETTIS

Internationally renowned art historian Salvatore Settis ignites a new debate about the Pearl of the Adriatic and cultural patrimony at large. In this fiery blend of history and cultural analysis, Settis argues that "hit-and-run" visitors are turning Venice and other landmark urban settings into shopping malls and theme parks. This is a passionate plea to secure the soul of Venice, written with consummate authority, wide-ranging erudition and élan.

THE MADONNA OF NOTRE DAME
BY ALEXIS RAGOUGNEAU

Fifty thousand people jam into Notre Dame Cathedral to celebrate the Feast of the Assumption. The next morning, a beautiful young woman clothed in white kneels at prayer in a cathedral side chapel. But when someone accidentally bumps against her, her body collapses. She has been murdered. This thrilling novel illuminates shadowy corners of the world's most famous cathedral, shedding light on good and evil with suspense, compassion and wry humor.

THE LAST WEYNFELDT
BY MARTIN SUTER

Adrian Weynfeldt is an art expert in an international auction house, a bachelor in his mid-fifties living in a grand Zurich apartment filled with costly paintings and antiques. Always correct and well-mannered, he's given up on love until one night—entirely out of character for him—Weynfeldt decides to take home a ravishing but unaccountable young woman and gets embroiled in an art forgery scheme that threatens his buttoned up existence. This refined page-turner moves behind elegant bourgeois facades into darker recesses of the heart.

MOVING THE PALACE
BY CHARIF MAJDALANI

A young Lebanese adventurer explores the wilds of Africa, encountering an eccentric English colonel in Sudan and enlisting in his service. In this lush chronicle of far-flung adventure, the military recruit crosses paths with a compatriot who has dismantled a sumptuous palace and is transporting it across the continent on a camel caravan. This is a captivating modern-day Odyssey in the tradition of Bruce Chatwin and Paul Theroux.

New Vessel Press

To purchase these titles and for more information
please visit newvesselpress.com.